Dead Dogs & Angels

Dead Dogs & Angels

by

Mickela Sonola

Holland House

www.hhousebooks.com

Paperback ISBN: 978-1-910688-39-7
Kindle: 978-1-910688-40-3

Cover design by Issara Edwards

Typeset by Polgarus Studio

Published in the USA and UK

Holland House Books
Holland House
47 Greenham Road
Newbury, Berkshire RG14 7HY
United Kingdom

www.hhousebooks.com

For
Carol and Goriola Sonola

1

About a week after Mama's funeral, Yinka woke up outside in the middle of the night. She looked up at the house, wiped the sticky mango leaves from her thighs and frowned.

This had happened before. Last time, she had woken up in the family car with the keys in the ignition. Her father, Thomas, had said

'Enough is Enough.'

and demanded that their houseboy fit a bolt high up on the front door, as if it had been him who had been found fast asleep in a car with the engine running.

You Africans, please listen to me as Africans

Yinka could hear the familiar rhythm of Fela Kuti's Afrobeat rumbling from a party a few streets away.

You Africans, please listen to me as Africans
And you non-Africans, listen to me with open mind
Suffer, suffer, suffer, suffer, suffer
Suffer for world
Na your fault be that
Me I say: na your fault be that

Dogs howled and barked in the street. Usually if they made this much noise at night the neighbours would rush out onto their balconies and driveways holding bush knives and spears or even shotguns. Mr Segun, who lived next door, preferred to use a bow and arrow. He was in his seventies and had cataracts; his eyes were a glassy blue-black. Yinka's father always said

"He waves his bow from his balcony, shouting at us to catch the thief and bring them to him for a good beating—" Then he would laugh so much that he could barely finish the sentence that always followed, "it's true, eh? In the land of the blind, the one-eyed man is king."

Almost all of the houses in the neighbourhood were surrounded by big walls or thick wire fences, and most were still being constructed. Yinka's home was the largest house on their street, and was surrounded by its own white-washed wall, pock-marked like honeycomb and topped with thick shards of broken glass. Bougainvillaea poured over it, fleshy shoots pushing through weakened patches of mortar and sprouting between the bricks and through to the other side. Towards the back but still within the yard's pink-and-white walls stood a small outhouse with a corrugated tin roof. It was occupied by two people: the Woles' house-maid Maryam and her uncle, Kehinde. Maryam mainly cleaned but would also cook sometimes, usually when Yinka's father was craving proper Yoruba food or when his wife was away. The rest of the time Yinka's mother cooked – boiled and boiled yam with gravy instead of soup, or meat soup with roasted and mashed yams and greens.

When her mother was at home, rice was to be eaten with a fork and not a spoon, and fried plantain or dodo, her favourite, with both a knife and a fork. Nothing was ever eaten with fingers in front of Yinka's mother. But when she was away in England they would eat eba and soup and dodo, rolling the eba in their fingers and dipping it into the sauce with the okra, the sound of her father's chewing silencing any notions of her mother's ideas of civilised dining.

Yinka turned to look at Maryam's house. There was a lamp burning, and she could see right in through the small window. Her mother said it was funny not to have curtains, that it would be like 'living inside a goldfish bowl'. Yinka did not think Maryam's house looked anything like a goldfish bowl. She hoped Maryam would be inside, but it didn't look like she was.

There was a van parked on one side of the small building, cloaked by an overgrown hibiscus shrub. Yinka shuffled carefully between the van and the wall and traced its scratched paintwork with her hand, feeling the dryness of the dust on her fingertips. Reaching the end, she noticed that the back door was slightly open and she peeked inside.

The copper coffee table that was usually in the centre of the living room sat next to the van's open door. Her father's record player, his Pride and Joy, was there as well and Yinka could see the shine of records peeking out of their sleeves to its side. Dumped on top of the table was the Molineux blender. The television and all their framed family photographs were shoved in a corner. It felt strange to see so much of her home squashed into this small space.

Yinka knew she should run back up to the house and wake her parents, but she also knew that being outside at night was sure to get her the Jobojobo. She could almost feel the familiar sting of the smooth thin wood on the back of her thighs. The beating itself would be over quickly; it was afterwards that the punishment really came, the swollen welts on her legs would show everyone that she had been bad again.

Maybe, if she could return some valuables, her father would forget all about her leaving the house at night. She would rescue her family's treasures and they'd all be Proud, even her mother. She would be a Good Girl.

She went first for the cream pile rug that was rolled up in the corner, but it was too heavy and its thick, wiry hairs got in her mouth. Wiping her tongue on her sleeve, she turned instead to her father's Pride and Joy. It was very heavy, but she hugged it close to her body and tiptoed towards the small dirty window. She stopped dead. Two men were coming straight for the van. She crouched down and made herself as small as possible, balancing the P and J on her knees. The coffee table was sharp against her back. She shut her eyes tightly and counted down from ten under her breath, hoping that when she finished she would wake up safely in her bed

"…four, three, two, one!"

but she was still in the van with her family's belongings. The vehicle was moving now, she could feel it crunching over the gravelled driveway. Yet the engine made no sound.

Suddenly she was scared. Within the compound's walls, she was free to play and roam around on her own. Now they were on the other side, where she was never allowed without an adult.

She was, as her mother often said when there was no one around but the two of them, in Deep Shit.

2

"Get in," a man's voice said from the front.

The door opened briefly then slammed shut and the engine burst into a deep rumble. Yinka felt the vehicle dip, and knew they had gone over the wide pothole at the end of their street. It took up half the road, her father had to drive on the wrong side to avoid it. The coffee table banged against her shin as the van turned right. Her father almost always went left – to go to work, to see Papa and Mama, to go to church. The only time they turned right was to take her mother to the airport.

The two men were talking but their voices were muffled by the grumble of the engine. The van sped up, and Yinka stretched out her legs and dug her heels into the floor's shallow ridges to brace herself while her family's belongings wobbled and clattered around her.

They would have guns, Yinka was sure. She had heard her father talking about Armed Robbery many times. He talked about it nearly as much as he did Corruption, but she didn't know what Corruption was. As she clung to the floor she remembered bits of stories about Armed Robbers. He had said that sometimes they robbed their victims while they slept, that other times families were stopped at fake police roadblocks and held with guns to their heads. Then, her mother said, if the family was unlucky the Armed Robbers would shoot the men and drag the women away to God Knows Where.

Yinka counted and counted and counted. She counted into the hundreds. Eventually she heard a plane coming in to land, growling like a thunderstorm gathering strength, and the van began to slow. She managed to get onto her hands and knees and crawl over to the window. Through it she could just about make out the road behind them, fading into the distance. They seemed to be driving down a narrow dirt track. The view through the window got darker and darker as thick heavy branches obscured the moonlight.

The engine spluttered and stopped and the front doors creaked and slammed. Yinka climbed carefully back over the coffee table and squeezed behind the rolled-up rug. When the back doors swung open she held her breath and pressed her body against it as tight as she could, but no one came inside. She shifted her position to see where the men had gone.

It was dark under the trees, but speckles of moonlight dripped through the canopy. The men went back and forth between the van and what looked like a small, flat-roof shed. There was a wavering glow from inside, and Yinka could smell kerosene. Briefly illuminated in the doorway, she saw a gun on the man's belt. He was Armed.

"Quickly, let's get everything inside," the Armed Man whispered. They pulled another load out of the very back of the van, but Yinka's hiding-place remained as yet untouched. Next they took the coffee-table and Yinka saw her chance. She crept out of her rug-hole, slid out, and quickly rolled under the van before they came back.

The Armed Man spoke again.

"Leave the records, I'll take them into the market today."

Both men stepped back inside the shed and began pushing things around.

Yinka took a deep breath and scrabbled out from under the van. Her pulse was throbbing so loud she was sure they would hear it. She looked down the track they had come up and could just make out the main road.

I can run, she thought, *I am the fastest runner in Class Six.*

She got into a runner's starting position, pulling away from the spindly crocked branches that reached out for her in the darkness.

I can run fast. Ready…

She held her breath.

Set…

She heard the thieves talking in broken English to one another. There was something familiar about one of their voices.

Go—

—but she wasn't ready to go. Squinting from the pressure of her air-filled cheeks, she looked down the track again.

What if the men catch me and drag me to God Knows Where?

Her father had said that at night the bushland would be full of snakes and bad spirits. That night is the time when evil spreads its wings and circles the earth. Her mother had said that that was a load of bloody rubbish.

"We've more to fear from the living than the dead." she'd said.

Yinka's breath finally escaped, hissing out of her mouth.

"Who's there?" the Armed Man shouted.

Yinka pushed herself further into the brush. Its witch-like fingers scratched through her pyjama shorts.

"Who's there?" he shouted again.

Yinka kept as still as she could. The man who had shouted was close, and she could see that he had a moustache. He pulled his gun out and waved it towards where she was hiding.

The other man walked over, shaking his head. It was Kehinde. She could tell by the laziness of his hips as he walked.

"Come out," the Armed Man said.

"Relax man, it's a goat or maybe a dog, stop shouting your mouth off," Kehinde said.

The Armed Man laughed.

"My mother would be happy with a wild goat to cook."

"You want the whole of Lagos to hear you? Keep quiet."

Kehinde's voice was low. He stayed where he was, a few steps behind the Armed Man.

"Now come on. Let's get on with this."

He turned and walked back, waving to the other to follow him.

The Armed Man kept his gun aimed toward the bush.

"Ah Kehinde, Big Man who likes play with little girls? You don't tell me what to do, stupid dog."

"Better than being an empty head," Kehinde said.

The Armed Man turned, pointing the gun towards Kehinde.

"Empty head, ah!" The Armed Man laughed and sucked his teeth. "Shut your mouth, it's my connections with the police that keep you from the firing squad, just remember that."

He turned quickly and fired into the bush. A spark of light splintered from the gun and Yinka pressed her body even harder into the earth and prayed that he wouldn't shoot again. Kehinde's tall frame suddenly appeared, looming over the other man. The sharp glint of a knife appeared against his throat and there was a sprinkling like raindrops splattering pitter-patter, on the leaves around her, on the ground, on her skin.

Kehinde bent down to pick up the gun. Then he dragged the man away to the sound of desperate gurgling, that got slowly quieter as they retreated into the darkness.

Yinka struggled through the brush on her hands and knees, imagining the spirits of the bushland grabbing at her feet and whipping her back and face. When there was finally room above her head she tried to run, but the bush would not let her. Tripping and scrambling she fought her way through until, finally, she tumbled forward and crashed head-first into a tree trunk. She had no breath or strength left inside her and her legs were as heavy as they were in her nightmares. She fell to her knees and threw up, again and again, until there was nothing left inside her but fear and pain and exhaustion.

She wiped her mouth with shaking hands and tried to stand, but her legs wobbled and she fell back down onto her knees. She could see a small clearing ahead of her and she pulled herself up and tottered towards it. Here, finally, the sky was visible above her. The moon was still glowing, just as it had when she'd looked up at it earlier only steps away from her own bed, as if nothing had happened since.

Her throat was sore and an acrid taste lingered bitterly in her mouth. Her skin felt hot and sticky, though the slight night breeze offered a little relief. The grasshoppers had turned up their nightly rattle, and cicadas clicked urgently in the trees. The familiar hum was comforting, it was her song of sleep.

Eventually she closed her eyes, and the world dipped into the darkness.

3

The call to prayer blasted from loudspeakers throughout Lagos, but Yusuf did not stir. He did not roll out his mat, did not join the chant that whispered through the city:

Allah u Akbar

This morning, Yusuf remained fast asleep.

He lived in a neglected storage room on the ground floor of the Wole house. The room was very bare. It contained no furniture and did not have its own toilet or sink. He slept on a mat on the concrete floor, next to which sat a worn copy of the Koran and a large tin cup. In one corner, he kept his few clothes: a spare pair of shorts, a long-sleeved shirt, and a pair of long trousers; in another, a paraffin lamp. The only other object in the room was a large tin bowl that sat in the crook between the door and the wall, which he used for washing.

From this makeshift home, Yusuf was able to hear every car that rolled past the house, was aware of every movement from the rooms above. He heard every harsh exchange, every slammed door, the double-bed's headboard's frantic knocking. Everything dripped down into his little echo chamber: giggles, moans, sighs and cries, shouts and steps and creaks.

Last night, however, he had not lain listening to other

people's lives. Last night, he had been out, living his own.

The music from the party stayed with him as he dreamed, deep, vibrant beats that danced around the steady pulse of his heart. Maryam, too, interrupted them, coming and going as though they belonged to her, teasing him.

When he finally woke, he sat up, pulled his knees to his chest, and wrapped his arms tightly around them. Only a few hours before these same arms and legs had been so close to hers, had even touched them, touched *her*.

Maryam had cut her hair. The five tightly-woven braids she usually wore were gone; in their place tight curls of her short afro had glistened with sweet-smelling coconut oil. He had wanted to reach over and stroke her skin where the oil had melted, down to the nape of her neck. Her clothes had not exposed too much of her body, not like the revealing American things on the other girls. She had worn a traditional blouse and wrap, and the fiery patterns had skimmed the contours of her curves as she'd moved to the relentless prompting of the drums. Watching her had switched him on, brought him to life. He had been able to feel each pulse of the bass, every individual tingle of sweat as it trickled down his skin. It was as though the music and the beat were part of him, of her, of them all.

They had smiled at each other as their bodies moved along to the rhythm. They were part of the room, part of the music, part of the throng of bodies dancing together.

Suffer, suffer,
Suffer, suffer...
Na your fault be that,
Me I say,
Na your fault be that

They had stopped only briefly, to eat cold fried plantain

and jollof rice and sip palm wine from plastic cups until the music drew them back into its rhythm.

Afterwards they walked back to the compound together and she planted a warm, sweet kiss on his lips.

He stretched his body slowly out again, lingering over this last part. Then he exhaled, carefully folded the memory up and put it away.

Usually in the mornings he would hear Yinka creeping about above him, little creakings on the floorboards as she walked around. Yesterday he had found her struggling with her bedsheet and helped her pull it off and turn the mattress over for her before her parents woke. On the days when Mr Wole did discover she had wet the bed, Yinka would be dragged back into her room, her face turned towards the wet stain.

"Look. Look at this. And you thought you could hide it." Then he would suck his teeth and grab Yinka by the ear. "How many times have we told you not to try to hide it, as if it's not bad enough that you are still wetting the bed?"

Yusuf would hang the mattress over the railings of the small balcony at the back of the house. He often loitered there, despite the smell of ammonia, to avoid having to watch Yinka being punished.

Yusuf reached for his tin cup and sipped from it. He was still tired, and his body ached from dancing. He rubbed his shaven head and listened. All was quiet. He rolled off his mat to prepare himself for prayer, trying to ignore the nagging thought that he might already have missed the call. He had never missed a dawn prayer. Not even when he had had malaria.

A strip of mid-morning brightness under his door caught his eye. He had definitely missed his prayers. Taking one last stretch, he stood, dressed, and went outside. The sun's glare caught him off-guard. The day was not as he usually greeted it, the air was warmer and more humid and on the road there were people shouting, dogs barking, a baby crying. There was something wrong, something absent. No sounds came from the house behind him.

The front door was not locked. At first he thought that it might have been left open accidentally, but Mr Wole would never leave his home unlocked, he was sure. From the kitchen he could see into the living room. There was no one there. Something was definitely not right. He picked up the bush knife that was kept in the pantry.

"Master?" he called out as he walked through the living room. There was something odd about the room. He noticed a pale patch on the floor – the rug was gone. Gone, too, was the coffee table with its copper map of Africa. He looked around. The records were all gone, and the record player with the cover that was so awkward to dust. The television was gone but its lopsided stand remained, permanently deformed by the weight it had held. The glass-fronted cabinet was still there, but all of the framed photographs that had stood proudly on its top were gone. It had been moved a little away from the wall – perhaps it had been too heavy to steal. Yusuf would sometimes press his face up to the photos when the family wasn't around. Mrs Wole and her three sisters, with their short square-shaped skirts and skinny white legs, the gold-framed photo of the couple standing on the church-steps on their wedding day, Mr Wole an inch shorter than his smiling wife, the two of them surrounded by confetti.

Yusuf rubbed the top of the cabinet with the palm of his hand. He had always thought it a sign of their wealth and prosperity to have their families displayed like that. He carried his own family's faces within him. Every contour and feature, each characteristic movement was carved forever into his memory. Like the way his late father had pinched at his nose whenever he was thinking over a problem, the way his mother covered her mouth when she smiled or was given a compliment.

The day he had left to find work in Lagos, his mother had been unwell. Her shrunken figure on the bed would forever be in his memory. It was just after midday and she had been resting.

"Mama, I am going," he had said.

She nodded in the darkness, not really at what he had said, but more in acknowledgement that he had spoken. He rested his hands on the bed next to her.

"Mama, I will come back when I can, I'll send money," he said. She opened her eyes and looked at him.

"Next time you come back, it will be to bury me."

She shrugged her shoulders and closed her eyes again.

"Ah, Mama."

"Go, that bus won't wait for you."

A pile of papers had fallen out of the cabinet. He knelt down and tried to shuffle them together, but more fell and joined them. Remembering that he was forbidden to open the cabinet, he abandoned the task and stood up. He took a long, deep breath, took a last look around the room, then made his way to the main bedroom and knocked on the door.

Softly, he called, "Master?"

He was relieved to hear Mrs Wole's voice a second later. "Bloody hell, Yusuf, what is it?" Then, more quietly, "Tom, Thomas, wake up."

Yusuf pushed the door open and stepped timidly inside. He had been in this room many times before, but never when the wife was still in bed. Mrs Wole must tidy the room before he came in in the mornings, he had never seen it like this. On the table at Mr Wole's side were a mug of tea with a fly buzzing around it and a half-drunk bottle of Fanta, and a pile of Mr Wole's clothes lay in a heap on the floor. On her side it was tidier, only the cotton shirt she'd worn the day before draped neatly over a chair.

"Go and dust something. What's wrong with you, boy?" Mr Wole snapped at him, one hand rubbing the sleep from his eyes, the other reaching for his glasses. Yusuf stepped closer to the bed. Mr Wole sat up, bare-chested and annoyed, while Mrs Wole remained wrapped in the sheets.

"Yusuf, go and do what you have been told!" Mr Wole shouted.

"Master, nothing to dust."

With this, Yusuf bowed his head apologetically and backed out of the room. He waited for them in the kitchen.

"Where the bloody hell is she then?" he heard Mrs Wole shout across the hall.

"Don't panic Jennifer, you're getting yourself in a state. We haven't checked with Maryam. Yusuf, go and see if Yinka is there," Mr Wole said.

"Phone the police, where's the phone? Yusuf, have you seen the phone?" Mrs Wole shouted.

"Missis, phone is gone," Yusuf stuttered.

"What are you waiting for, boy?" This came from Mr Wole.

"Yes, Sir." Yusuf hurried out of the kitchen, only then remembering the bush knife he still held in his hand. He slipped it back into the pantry and stepped out into the yard. If only he had not overslept. Yinka was usually the first of the family awake, and would often come and join him as he swept the kitchen or the steps outside. She had probably gone to find some mischief, he thought, smiling. He hoped that Mr Wole would not give her Jobojobo when they found her.

His heart began to beat faster as he approached Maryam's house. He thought of her lips and whether she would let him kiss her again as she had last night.

4

When the two men in smart woollen suits had finished questioning Thomas, they shook their heads.

"Robbers are always armed these days. She probably disturbed them while they were at work..." The man's voice trailed off. His partner stood silently next to him staring at his shoes, with sweat soaking the collar of his shirt.

They went to find a phone they could borrow and to begin organising a search-party. Thomas watched them from his window as they passed Yinka's photograph around the other officers and neighbours who had gathered to help look for her.

When was the last time he had looked at her? Not just a glance, but properly looked, like he had done when she was a baby lying in his lap? They had spent hours like that. She had been a quiet, contented baby. He knew exactly what her baby-face had looked like. But when the police had asked him to describe her as she was now, he had struggled. He had pulled out an envelope of photographs and negatives from a drawer in the kitchen and tipped them onto the table, flicking impatiently through, searching for the right one. He was taking too long but nothing seemed right, to show what she looked like. Her almond shaped eyes were dark, like pools of oil, a stark contrast to the lightness of her skin. His sister-in-law had described her as the colour of warm milky Horlicks. He didn't have time for culinary descriptions of people, this was more common with his English relatives. Coffee, cocoa, chocolate, now milky Horlicks. He focused on the picture in front of him; it had been taken shortly after they had arrived in Nigeria. He had taken many of her wearing her traditional dress that day, so Jennifer could send them back to her family in England. Her head was wrapped in a plain blue gele, she was dressed for church. It had started to unravel to expose her wispy, curly hair as soon as the service began. She was so skinny.

Is. She is.

He felt a wave of irritation as the man roughly examined the photograph, pressing his thumbs and fingers on the glossy paper.

The police outside began splintering off, taking groups of neighbours with them. Thomas' head throbbed. He closed his eyes and tried to pray, but the words seemed far away, just beyond his reach. He knew his mother would have found the words.

"Mama. Keep her safe," he whispered under his breath.

He rubbed his Adam's apple as if this might somehow release the tight knot of worry that swelled in his throat. The odour of rotting faeces crept up his nostrils, a familiar smell. When they had first arrived at Ikeja, the land next to their apartment had been a wasteland. A large sign had promised the erection of luxury apartments in which Thomas, at one time, had hoped to invest. But the developer had got rich elsewhere and lost interest; the barren land had become a dumping-ground. A place where the people who lived opposite them defecated because their bathrooms had been ripped out to make room for more beds. A place where the same families' children, with their bulging bellies and umbilical hernias, played happily. Even now they were down there dancing about in it, weaving in and out of the adults. Thomas looked more closely at them. Today they seemed somehow different. Or perhaps today it was he who was different. Today he did not feel pity for them, didn't thank God that Yinka was not among them. Today he would have given anything for her to be down there, where he could see her.

"Tom, I can't sit here, just waiting. I can't...I'm going out to look for her."

Jennifer had dragged herself up from her chair and was now leant awkwardly against the screen door. Her eyes wouldn't rest on his, they darted about, seeing everything, focusing on nothing.

"We have to stay here," he said gently.

"God! It's typical of you. Just typical. My daughter is God knows where and all you can do is...bloody..."

She was shaking. Tom took one long stride and he was next to her, holding her to his chest.

"Jennifer, the police – no, the whole of Ikeja – is searching for her," he said. She pulled away.

"But what if they don't and we're sitting here. I don't know if I'll ever forgive myself if anything has..."

Her voice faltered and she wrapped her fingers around the arm of the chair, gripping so hard that her knuckles turned white.

"Don't do this, it's not your fault. Come, let's stand out on the balcony, get some fresh air—"

"I want my baby."

"Come on." He took her hand and led her out through the netted doorway. "She needs us here. We need to be strong, we have to be here, in case..."

5

From the balcony she could hear Tom making tea. Footsteps in the kitchen, creaking cupboard doors, crockery against wood. Something else… was he humming? Could he be humming at a time like this? She stood up, walked to the balcony, and looked down to the road.

This morning she had gone to Maryam's house almost certain that Yinka wouldn't be there. But the idea of seeing Maryam felt so comfortable, so normal, that she went there first anyway. She had almost wanted to sit down, chat first, be offered a drink, politely decline… anything, anything at all, to delay being faced with reality, to delay being told that her daughter was not there, that Maryam did not know where she was.

Although Yinka was in and out of Maryam's little house as if it were her own, Jennifer had rarely been inside it. She strode through the main room, noticing how the canopy of mango trees kept the interior pleasantly cool despite the heat outside. In the kitchen there was a table with four wooden chairs around it, and a wooden bowl holding a few old bananas and a couple of green mangoes still attached to their branch. A few books, most of which she recognised as her own, lay in a pile on one side. Yinka must have brought these here.

She tried to pace herself, to look around first, take in the details, but the question just slipped out. As soon as it had been said she realised she didn't want to hear the answer. Had she even waited for Maryam to reply? She couldn't remember hearing the poor girl speak, couldn't remember leaving. She found herself back in her own house, with Thomas looking at her fretfully.

"Mr Segun has called the police, they are on the way over," he'd said, glancing past her, just in case.

"Perhaps she's scared. Frightened. Maybe the robbers scared her and she's lying somewhere frightened. She could have knocked her head…"

Jennifer had run into Yinka's 's bedroom, looking under the bed, in the wardrobe, under boxes and toys, throwing things left and right. Breathless, she stopped and looked out of the window. A man in an open shirt was wandering through the rubbish, picking up and sifting through bags. As she watched, he stood, opened his fly, and relieved himself, indifferent to any potential observers.

She had then run through the house to the fire-escape staircase.

"Yinka!" she shouted.

Only her own echo had replied.

Zombie-like, she had walked back through the house. The policemen were already there, and she had shaken their hands, noticing their flashy well-fitted suits, the thick wool weave unsuitable for the Lagos heat. Only big bribes could pay for that sort of thing. How much would it cost to get Yinka back? The ransom, the police? What if they didn't have enough?

What if they didn't have enough?

She had gone to sit down then decided instead to make herself another cup of tea. She was hungry and her stomach was already swishing uncomfortably with all the tea she'd already drunk, but she didn't want to think about eating. What kind of mother sat and filled her stomach with food while her child was missing?

Yusuf appeared with a cup of tea and placed it next to her. The boy had a knack for appearing out of nowhere – and yet where had he been last night?

"Have the police spoken to you?"

Again, the words tumbled out on their own.

He had nodded and looked down at his feet. She didn't want to think it, but she couldn't help it. They trusted him.

They had had a driver once, she couldn't remember his name. Tom had given him money to take to a friend in Ibadan. Two hundred Naira. Tom, eyes to the floor and disappointment weighing his body down, had said it had been his own fault, he should never have put the money in his charge. How could a boy like that not take it and run?

"The boy should never have been put in that position," Tom had said.

She had listened, but only found herself irritated by the way he pronounced the 'L' in should. Two hundred Naira was a lot of money. The boy had been part of the household. She had even bought him a Christmas present, to his apparent astonishment.

"Where's his loyalty? All that we've done for him."

Thomas had shrugged and said, "You can't eat loyalty."

Jennifer snapped, then.

"You can wave goodbye to two hundred Naira, just like that, and rant at the cost of a yam at the market."

"But Jennifer, that's the point, isn't it?"

"Oh, don't start getting on your soapbox…"

Thomas had sighed, and that had been that.

Yusuf had bent to pick up the empty mugs. Without looking up at her, he'd said,

"Missis?"

"Yes, Yusuf."

"Missis, notin to clean. I help police? Notin to clean."

"Where were you last night?"

"At a party, with Maryam."

She had moved closer to him. "Where? Where was this party?"

"At the musician's compound. Five, ten minutes' walk, up towards the school. I get permission from Mr Wole. I ask if it is OK that I take Maryam. You ask Mr Wole." The tone of his voice had risen and he sniffed away the tears that were gathering behind his eyes.

"Sorry Missis."

"Yes, okay, go."

Then she had walked back out onto the balcony. Thomas, still humming quietly to himself, joined her outside.

"What I cannot understand," – he spoke as though midway through a conversation – "is how the door was left unlocked. You know I am vigilant about security. Did you check the locks before you went to bed?" He did not look at her.

"What? What? Are you saying that I forgot to lock the door? That it's my fault?" She was trembling now. It hadn't occurred to her that the door had been left unlocked. Had she locked the door behind her before she went back to bed?

"No, I'm not accusing you, Jennifer. I just can't understand how thieves managed to break in to the house and I didn't even wake up," Thomas said. "How could I have slept through my own daughter being taken?"

She stood next to him and placed her hand on top of his, curling the tips of her fingers under his. "Why is this happening to us?"

There was a pleading in her voice, as though she hoped that he would tell her that it wasn't at all, that it was all a terrible dream. That soon she would wake up and Yinka would be there by the bed, tapping her on the shoulder, saying

"Mummy, mummy, I'm hungry,"

and she would shuffle over in the bed and pat the sheet next to her and Yinka would slide in and wrap her thin, downy arms around her. When was the last time she had done that? When was the last time she had wanted Yinka's touch? All she could think of now were all the times, over the last few days, that Yinka had come to her and she had pushed her away.

It wasn't just because of the funeral, either. It started before that, before she had gone back home. Somehow, the more Yinka grew, the more irritating Jennifer found her. Her constant questioning, her growing defiance. Never in front of Thomas, though, oh no. Never in front of Daddy. Thinking about it properly, she wondered what it had really been that irked her, what had actually changed? If she was honest with herself, was it Yinka at all? Or was it really more the frustration, every month, when her period arrived? Her mother-in-law's constant nagging? Yinka was growing up, and losing her baby fat. Her ankles and wrists were thinning, her face was changing.

Jennifer thought back to the first time she had turned up at Tom's lodgings. She'd knocked and a Nigerian woman in traditional dress had come to the door, looked Jennifer up and down, and loudly sucked her teeth before calling out to

Tom in Yoruba. They had caught a bus and walked through Hyde Park. Even in the freezing cold, tourists formed long queues for the open-top bus tours around London. They had held hands. He was talking too much. He had taken her to see a film at a theatre near where he lived.

They were sitting on a bench and watching the ducks waddling across the Serpentine's thin layer of ice when she had blurted out that she was pregnant. She'd held her breath, expecting him to walk away. He got up, walked towards the lake and threw a stone at the ice. Then, after a second, he came back and sat with her and said

"The baby, it's your boyfriend's, the one at the party."

"Well, he was my boyfriend," she said, looking down.

"He won't marry you?"

She shrugged. "I didn't hang around to find out. He doesn't know."

"You must tell him."

She had turned to face him then. "I don't want to be with him."

Jennifer didn't cry, even that day, as they sat in the bitter cold, when Thomas embraced her. She had kept her head up, tears stinging her eyes although she had not cried. She never cried.

That was the day he asked her to marry him.

Later, he had insisted on catching the bus with her and walking her home.

"I want you to know that the way I treat you tonight will be the way I'll always treat you," he said.

After they were married, Thomas told his parents that his English wife was pregnant. Jennifer surrendered the collection of girl's names she had gathered through her childhood: Katherine, Emily, Annabelle, Audrey. Sitting down in the musty registrar's office at the Town Hall with her one-month-old baby sleeping on her lap, she had taken a deep breath and said:

'Yinka, Yinka Wole'.

6

The dawn air was cool. Yinka woke shivering, curled up in a ball with a thin mist of dew tingling on her skin. Her fingernails were black, her knuckles bloodied and her elbows grazed. She followed the scratches up her legs with her finger; above her knee they met a deeper gouge that tore up her thigh. As she prodded the sensitive flesh, a red ant crawled up in between her toes and took a bite. She flicked it off and squashed it with her nail, only to feel another and another crawl back in its place. She jumped up and stamped her feet on the ground, frantically brushing them off with her hands.

The oranges and reds of the morning sky dripped in through the gaps in the canopy. Yinka's throat was dry and raw, and her bladder was so full it was painful. She pulled her shorts down and squatted. The hot stream caught her ankle and burnt at the broken skin. She cried silently, afraid to let out a sound in case she was heard. She was thirsty and hungry and scared.

She managed to get herself up and shuffled towards the taller trees at the edge of the semi-clearing, then stopped. She thought this was the way she had come in, but was now scared to re-enter the darkness. Ahead of her all she could see was shadows; shadows that seemed to move all on their own, dancing around like ghostly figures.

Where am I?

She looked up at the sky. She knew she would need to track the sun as it rose in order to find her way back. It was going to get hotter and with the heat would come the mugginess, stifling and close.

First, though, she had to go back in the direction she'd come from, back to the wooden shack. Then she would be able to find her way back onto the road. What if Kehinde was still there?

Kehinde had always been nice to her, especially when her mother was away and Mama was ill. He would come and spend time with her when she had no one else to talk to.

Her parents did not like him.

"Never trust a man with his eyes too close together," Mummy had said.

"He's lazy, Good for Nothing," Daddy had said. He had, however, also said this about her if she had not kept her room Clean and Tidy.

Kehinde had said she was pretty.

When she couldn't be with Mama, she would spend the afternoon hours on the balcony, watching the children playing on the street below. Or sitting under the house, playing in the dust; drilling holes in the ground with her fingers for the tiny ants to disappear into.

Kehinde would come and join her and give her money and sweets.

At first, she'd said, "I'm not allowed to take money from strangers."

"Well, I'm not a stranger," he said, hand still stretched out.

Her hands remained at her side.

He'd shrugged his shoulders and smiled.

"Okay," she said, and taken the money.

When he'd gone, she ran up the stairs and deposited the now-warm coins in her pink and white piggy-bank. After that, Kehinde often gave her presents: sometimes it would be a boiled sweet wrapped like a Christmas cracker or a bottle of Coca-Cola, and once even a fifty Kobo piece. She would crunch down quickly on the sweets, swallowing the sharp sugary fragments and picking the sticky remains out of her teeth. She didn't tell anyone about Kehinde's gifts, not even Mama.

After a while, she began to get a curdled-milk feeling in her stomach when she saw him walking down the street in her direction, though she wasn't sure why. She tried to ignore it, and would run eagerly down to open the gate for him and walk with him to the back of the compound. Sometimes he would reach up and pull a mango from the tree for her. He would ask her about school and she would answer, hopping on the spot, waiting for him to dig into his pockets for loose change or sweets. Sometimes he would stroke her hair. She was used to the painful tugs and pulls from the afro comb scratching her scalp as Aunty Modupe combed her hair. His touch was soft and slight, his fingers would travel down and tickle her neck, and that felt nice. Soon she looked forward to his caresses as much as she did the dirty copper coins and sticky sweets that he gave her, despite the funny feeling in her tummy.

Sometimes he would come back with a friend. They would drift into the yard with their shirts hanging open. They'd sit on the plastic chairs at the back of the compound under the mango trees and drink beer and smoke Kool cigarettes. They talked noisily, laughing and drinking late into the night. Her mother would get annoyed when they did that, especially as their voices rose as the night went on. This happened most Fridays. Maryam was paid on Fridays. On Saturday mornings Maryam would clear up the discarded bottles and cigarette-ends from the yard.

Then she remembered Kehinde standing over the body of the Armed Man.

Flies gathered around her, sticking to her sweat and settling on the gobs of drying blood on her arms and legs. She waved them away and looked up at the sky.

Often at home she would stand on her balcony and watch the sunrise. If she wanted to watch it set, she had to go to the back of the house. The sun set the same direction as the airport, and she liked to watch the planes fly in and out of the orange-red clouds. Yinka thought that if she walked towards the sunrise, away from the airport, then she would get home.

'Never, Eat, Shredded, Wheat. North, East, South, West.'

She brushed herself off, being careful not the catch any of the scabs that had begun to crust on her skin. She looked down at her feet. They were cut and grazed, but her soles were thick from walking without shoes so much.

I'll walk home.

Following the direction the sun had risen from, she walked into the brush, leaving the light of the clearing behind. Stepping over the sharp branches and mounds of damp leaves and mud, she would have given anything for the shoes she usually hated wearing.

The light was dim amongst the trees, and it was hot there. Sweat dripped down her body and mosquitoes buzzed around her. After a while her determination began to fade and she wished that she had waited in the clearing for someone to find her. She could still see the sky through the leaves and branches, but the sun was not so clear. When she looked around she could not tell exactly which direction she had come from. Everything seemed to look like everything else. Insects would gather whenever she stopped so she hurried on, slapping her arms and face. She began to think of the other creatures she knew of that lived in the bush, poisonous snakes and spiders, bush pigs with huge, dangerous tusks. She picked up a long stick and swept it in front of her as she'd seen Yusuf do when he was cutting the grass with his bush knife. Yusuf had warned her about the grass that grew tall at the back of the compound,

"Don't you play back there. That's where the snakes hide, okay?"

Despite Yusuf's regular cutting it grew fast, and when it was long she would always avoid going into the back of the yard.

When she had gone to bed the night before, Daddy was too tired to read her a bedtime story. Usually he'd read one of her Ladybird books and afterwards he'd sing a prayer and she would join in with his "Amen" at the end with her sing-song voice. Sometimes he told her stories that Mama had told him when he was a child instead.

"Did *your* daddy read to you when you were little?" Yinka had asked.

"No. We rolled out our mats, said our prayers and went to sleep"

"You slept on a mat?"

"Everyone slept on mats."

"Did you say the same prayer as we do?"

"No, we recited the Lord's Prayer."

"That's what we say at roll-call at school."

"Time for bed."

"Tell me one of Mama's stories,"

"Not tonight, Yinka."

She slipped down onto her pillow and he kissed her.

"Goodnight, Yinka"

"Is mummy coming in?" she had asked, sitting up again.

"Mummy's tired," he said, and kissed her again.

When he had shut the door behind him, she closed her eyes and tried to remember a story by herself. The stories her father told never started with 'Once upon a time', and they never ended with 'happily ever after'. Now as she walked, sore-footed with stick in hand, she decided to tell herself a story.

Olu and Tunde were best friends, but very different boys. Olu was quiet and content to play, while Tunde was brash and loud. Tunde was a clever boy, but contrary. If he felt like it he would argue that black was white and white was black.

One day a very well-known storyteller came to visit the boys' village. It was said that he was older than Methuselah himself and at least as wise. Word spread, and soon the whole village had gathered to hear him speak.

The storyteller told the tale of a creature; born of woman, but not human in its nature. The villagers sat in silence as he described how this beast had the ability to jump between the living and the spirit realms at will; how it could change its shape to whatever animal it wished.

Through the silence, a loud tooth-sucking rang.

"That can't be true."

It was Tunde who said this.

The young boy was not only challenging the man who was older than Methuselah himself but he was also accusing him of lying. This was very serious.

Despite the interruption, the storyteller went on, his wise smile unmoved. Tunde smiled as well – he believed he had beaten the old man. The rest of the parents watched their transfixed children proudly, but not Tunde's mother. Her head was bowed in shame, and there was sadness in her eyes.

Tunde interrupted two or three times more, but the wise old man seemed not to hear.

When the story was finished, the people scattered to prepare a huge feast. All but Tunde's parents, who knew they must stay and apologise. The storyteller was very angry and spoke first, banging his long staff on the ground;

"If you cannot teach your son respect, I shall have to. Your son wants to see – and so I will show him."

Tunde's mother began to cry. A cloud swept over the village and its people that night, but what could be done?

Tunde was never seen by any of them again.

When Olu was a grown man with his own children, the wise old storyteller returned, and the village gathered once again to hear his stories. As he listened, Olu waited; he wanted to ask the old man what had happened to his friend. When the end of his story came, however, the storyteller answered for him. Bending down low, so low that the children at the front could feel the hairs on his beard, he said;

"And if you don't believe me, go deep into the bush and ask Tunde."

Yinka was beginning to catch glimpses of pale blue sky and bright white light piercing through the trees. It was even hotter and more humid now. Her cheeks felt hot and swollen and her clothes clung to her body. She itched all over, it felt as though a thousand ants were trying to get out from under her skin. Sweat burnt at her tired eyes and stung at her scratches.

She was out of breath but she kept on moving, even as the bushes got dense again. On and on she traipsed in the direction she thought the sun had risen from, sure that it was the same sun that burned above her house, sure that it would eventually lead her home.

The wet season was supposed to have begun, although there hadn't been any rain. The humidity rose expectantly. No relief came. Walking determinedly on, she took her mind back to a day the week before, back to her home and back to safety.

As usual since Mama had gone to hospital, she had been sitting and watching the world outside the compound's white-washed walls: the women with their baskets of food and crates of chickens, stopping to wipe their foreheads with the backs of their hands or the edges of their blouses, making their slow way home from the market, the long, thin men who seemed to grow out of the horizon, carrying huge buckets of water, balancing them on rods or on top of their heads, the younger boys resting on upside-down crates, lazily fanning themselves with newspapers. The street was quieter in the afternoon; even the children across the road who didn't have to go to school were subdued by the heat.

While Maryam cooked food in the kitchen, while Yusuf fought the traffic to pick her father up or get more water, Yinka sat and waited and watched. Only when the phone rang would she move. When that happened she would jump straight up and rush into the living room to pick it up first, knowing it would be her mother.

"I miss you Mummy. When are you coming home?" she said on this particular day, pressing the phone to her ear, listening for the faraway echo of her mother's voice.

"Soon. How's Mama? Are you being good while I'm

away?" asked the voice, from the bottom of the deepest well.

"Mama is very sick and there's been no rain and Aunty Modupe cries all the time," Yinka shouted down the phone.

"It's pouring here," her mother said.

"Everyone is praying for Mama to get better and for it to rain."

Mama Wole had not got better.

Yinka brought herself back. She did not want to think about Mama. She walked towards the sun and tried to think instead of what it would lead her to: Mummy and Daddy and Home. The bush was now becoming dense and overgrown and her skin got caught on the branches as she made her way through. The mud was no longer visible beneath the sticks and the leaves and she was scared. It felt like the bush was closing in, like it was a living, breathing creature that would swallow her up if she wasn't careful. Suddenly she couldn't bear the itchiness and she jumped up and down scratching everywhere, her shins, chest, arms and cheeks, clawing at her back until the itching was joined by a pain too great to continue. There was fresh blood on her bitten-down nails where she had scratched at half-formed scabs.

"Mummy, Daddy," she whispered.

Then a surge of panic rose up from the pit of her stomach and she could hear herself but it didn't feel like it was her, screaming, "I'm here! I'm here!" over and over until her voice was hoarse and she couldn't scream anymore. Still no one came. Her hands and feet were sore from stomping and pulling and tearing and her legs ached.

When no more sound would come from her throat she lay down, too exhausted even to cry any more.

7

Maryam had sat on the concrete step and watched as Yusuf disappeared into his room. She knew that her uncle and his friend would by then already have robbed the Wole's house. Then she had taken off her sandals and crept inside, pausing, breath held, outside her uncle's silent room and peeking inside: it was empty.

She had uncurled the threadbare mat in her corner of the main room and lain down without undressing, tired but sure that she would not sleep. The familiar smells of burlap bags, sweet onions and earthy yams were comforting, and she closed her eyes and allowed herself to sink into her thoughts. She had thought mostly of Yusuf, and of the first and probably the last party that she would ever attend. As she drifted she stroked at the thick weave of the blouse she wore, one of the very few of her late mother's possessions she had managed to keep from Kehinde's greedy hands.

After serving dinner to the Woles, Maryam had waited outside Yusuf's door. When he saw her, his eyes widened. She covered a smile behind her hand.

"The Woles have gone to bed?"

"Yes, the missis was very tired."

"Perhaps I should go—"

"Ah, come on, they won't thank you for waking them

up. Besides, the door will be locked by now."

She had walked towards the gate, and held her hand out for him to hold.

They had been able to hear the music from the party long before they reached the top of the road. She squeezed his hand. She could not remember a time that she had ever felt so alive. The drummers' poundings reverberated around them, through them, sinking into her flesh, into her bones, filling her up.

They had danced, both leading and following one another. She remembered the sweat – sweat dripping down her back and underneath her breasts, sweat everywhere. The good kind of sweat, sweet-smelling and salty, the kind of sweat that means you are alive.

A line of women had trooped out into the yard carrying trays laden with pots and bowls of steaming food. Yusuf pulled her from the frantic dancing to watch the food being set down and unwrapped. There had been so much: fried plantain, whole fish, soups and piles of jollof rice and pyramids of moin-moin wrapped in palm leaves. Maryam filled two plates and they ate in silence, watching as more people joined the party.

"Are you tired?" Yusuf had asked as he scooped the last of the rice from his plate.

"A little."

"Let's go, it's nearly two-thirty."

"One more dance?"

Maryam rushed ahead to open the gate so that Yusuf would not notice the broken padlock. She had felt glad of the palm wine as she pretended to lock it behind him, it dampened the guilt she knew she ought to have felt.

"Thank you for inviting me," he had said as they approached his room. "It was a shock, but I am glad. You know, I like you, but I fear your uncle."

"He's away tonight," she said. "I like you too."

Yusuf had looked anxiously up at the house.

"They won't wake up."

Then he closed his eyes and leaned in to kiss her. She had kept her own eyes open. His face blurred for a second before his lips and body pressed against hers. She had seen pictures of lovers kissing on the front of Mrs Wole's books. She waited, expecting him to grab at her breasts or try to lift up her skirt, but he hadn't. She wanted to please him. She pressed her hand against his groin, but he pulled away.

"Goodnight, Maryam," he had said and kissed her again, this time so lightly she barely felt it.

"I really like you."

Maryam had fallen asleep replaying the scene over and over. She did not sleep for long, and was awake long before the call to prayer broadcast at five. She changed out of her dress and made a sweet coffee and waited.

She was still waiting when the screen door rattled and Mrs Wole's voice rang loud through the house.

"Yinka? Yinka!"

Maryam opened the screen door and Mrs Wole rushed in, still wearing her bedclothes. She looked frantically around.

"Is she here?"

"Yinka? No Missis?"

"We've been robbed. She's got to be here."

"She's not here," Maryam said.

Mrs Wole ran out, still calling the little girl's name.

Yusuf arrived immediately after. His forehead was creased with worry, as though the child was his own.

"She's hiding somewhere. Don't be worried about that cheeky kid," she said.

"Maryam, Yinka is missing. Their house was robbed last night while we were at the party. Everything was taken."

"The girl is around some place, thieves aren't going to take some little picken."

"Come help me look around." He was already walking away.

She reached for the broom and started to sweep the narrow porch.

"I should stay, in case she comes here. Perhaps she's hiding from the Jobojobo."

"No, I don't think so," Yusuf said, doubtfully. "Okay, you wait here." He stopped. "You look sick."

"I'm okay," she said, lingering in the doorway, willing him to run back and put his arm around her waist and kiss her again like he had done the night before.

"Last night was…good," she said.

"I'd better go."

Maryam called after him, "That girl wakes up early you know, she probably saw the place was empty and got frightened."

Maryam bent into the broom, quickly brushing the clouds of dust off the porch and onto the ground, and the warm feeling that had fluttered in her chest at seeing Yusuf sank slowly into her stomach and soured.

8

Yusuf walked around the compound.

"First they bury her grandmother, and now Yinka disappears."

He went to the back of the building to check the water tank. It had been filled to the rim less than three months ago, and the disused pipes had grumbled into life. The compound then had running water for a month, before the pipes had groaned again and the water became thick with brown sediment. They had gone back to getting their water by the bucketful in the early mornings from the hawkers who shouted as they passed. Sometimes Yusuf would help Mr Wole to fill bottles up at the pharmacy where he worked. No matter how often or how quickly he tried to fill them, there was never enough.

While Mrs Wole had been in England they filled their water at the grandparents' house. Yusuf would drive Yinka there after school, and when they arrived she would jump out of the car and open the gate for him to drive through, hopping from one freshly-bare foot to the other on the hot stones. Her grandmother would always be standing in the shade of the house, waiting for her.

"Yinka, where are your shoes?"

Yinka would ignore the question and rush past her,

disappearing into the cool darkness of the house. Yusuf noticed each time how the old woman had to lean for a moment against the doorframe. She seemed to have aged twenty years in that single month.

Modupe would always be in the kitchen preparing food and hovering over her mother, chastising Yinka when she became too loud or boisterous, and threatening her with Jobojobo. Yinka would snatch sly glances at the long thin canes that leaned against the wall next to her grandfather's easy chair. At four o' clock Yusuf would go back into Lagos to pick Mr Wole up from work and bring him for the evening meal at their grandparent's house.

Yusuf always ate in the kitchen after he had cleared the table. While they were eating he would quietly wash up the saucepans and sweep the kitchen floor. Sometimes the door to the dining room was left slightly ajar, just enough for him to hear the family begin their meal with a Christian prayer and to see them eating. One particular day, there was no talk to follow, no news or debate. They ate in silence – even Yinka was subdued as she rolled her eba in little balls with her fingers and submerged them in chopped okra before dipping them into the pepper sauce. Mr Wole, who usually teased Yinka about eating too much dodo, or, more recently, chattered endlessly about President Obasanjo, was silent also. He stared at his plate, occasionally glancing at his mother, whose own plate never seemed to go down.

After a while, Papa Wole took an orange from the fruit bowl and made a crater in the top with his thumbnail. He peeled the thick skin away and gathered it into the palm of his hand, passing the segments to his wife with the other. Yusuf watched as she slipped them tenderly into her mouth.

Mr Wole said, "Mama, you're not hungry?"

Modupe said, "She's not been eating. Look how thin she

is, Papa. If she's not going to tell us, you must."

Mama Wole turned towards the door of the kitchen.

"Yusuf, you know the British have a saying that eavesdroppers hear nothing good about themselves. Come and clear these dishes and take Yinka outside to play."

He slipped into the dining room with his head bowed. Yinka jumped straight off her seat as he came in, rocking the table in her excitement at being excused.

That evening the old woman was rushed to the hospital. She never came home again.

Yusuf lay on his belly and leaned in further under the water tank, while at the same time lifting the lid as high as he could to let in the light. A few inches of stagnant water settled at the bottom. He was both relieved and disappointed that she wasn't inside. The sound of the falling lid startled one of the policemen, who had stopped to take a Fanta out of the nearby ice-box. He frowned at Yusuf, holding him in a stare until Yusuf turned away. He looked towards the back of the compound, hoping to see Maryam. Maryam had not seemed to be concerned that Yinka was gone, which he thought was strange. He took a step to head down the path, then shook his head and instead walked out of the compound. Taking the narrow tracks between the houses, he added his own voice to the others that echoed in the neighbourhood, calling for the little girl.

By the time the call to prayer sang through the air at midday he was back at the compound, shirt soaked in sweat and his body aching with worry. He looked up, but he ignored the call. Mr and Mrs Wole were by the gate and gathered on the road were some neighbours and a few policemen. Mrs Wole saw Yusuf as he approached, but seeing that he was alone she looked quickly away again.

"We're running out of drinks and biscuits," Mr Wole said to Yusuf. "Take the car and get some more from Albert's store. Make sure the drinks are cold and don't let him sell you soft biscuits."

Yusuf held out his hand for the car key but Mr Wole had already softened his voice and turned to his wife.

"I've called the doctor for you."

"What did you do that for?" she said.

"I was worried, all this stress."

"For the love of God Tom, I don't need a bloody doctor, can *he* find my daughter?" she said, and Mr Wole winced.

"Perhaps he can help you."

"Help me, how? With one of his magic pills? You'd like that wouldn't you, you stupid little man."

"Jennifer!" Mr Wole turned to Yusuf. "Big ears, what are you still standing there for?"

"Car keys," Yusuf stammered. Mr Wole threw the keys at him.

"Straight there and back."

As Yusuf reversed out of the driveway, he saw Mr Wole rushing up the stairs after his wife.

9

Yinka was still too exhausted to cry. She sat cross-legged, staring down at her grazed legs, and gently pressed down on the tacky scab that had started to form on the deep cut on her thigh. Then she squinted up at the sky and whispered croakily,

"What's the time Mr Wolf?"

"Time to get up and walk," said a voice. It must have come from inside her head but it sounded as real as her own, and so much like Mama's that she jumped up and looked around – but there was no one there.

She picked up her stick and squinted up at the sun again. It was high, almost directly above her head.

"Twelve o'clock," she said.

She had played this game with her cousins when she lived in England, but there was no one to play with in their new home. She was not allowed to run around with the other kids on their street because her father said that they were Not Of Her Calibre. So, she played on her own, on the balcony or in the backyard. Sometimes she would act out stories from her Ladybird books, jumping around, changing from one character to another: Little Red Riding Hood, Cinderella, Gretel, Rose Red and Rose White. When it was too hot to play, she would lie down in the shade and pretend to be

Sleeping Beauty, excitement tingling at the bottom of her tummy as she waited for the Prince's kiss.

If she had had some crumbs she could have left a trail for Mummy and Daddy. She decided she would have to be the Woodcutter Prince instead. Her stick became a hefty sword, and she began forging her way through the thorns and vines.

"My! What big teeth you have!"

"All the better to eat you with!"

She sliced through imaginary wolf's imaginary stomach and Mama stepped out of its hollowed body and squeezed Yinka ever so tight, just like she used to before she got sick, the way she always had whenever Yinka cried. Yinka's eyes pricked a little then, but she did not cry again.

She walked on, ignoring the sweat that dripped down her back and sides. She had grown accustomed to the stifling heat since moving to Lagos. When her mother hung their washing out she would wipe her face with her shirt.

"You'd be better off steaming veg out here," she would say.

Yinka was thirsty and her lips were dry and cracked, while her body was drenched with sweat. She stopped and glanced around, hoping to find a fruit tree she recognised, like the ones that grew in her backyard. Everything here looked strange and unfamiliar, though, and she couldn't risk eating something poisonous. Flies swarmed and buzzed around her face but she was too tired to fight them.

She took a long breath, called out, "Two o'clock!" and began moving forward again.

Then, suddenly, she heard it. Loud and Clear, as Daddy would say: a rustling behind her, as if something or someone was following her. Unsure what to do, she trudged on through the undergrowth. When she stopped to scratch her itchy, bitten feet, the movement behind her also stopped. She turned around.

Nothing.

Ahead of her there was a giant tree, more broad than tall, with a trunk that looked big enough for her to hide inside. She ran for it. The hole seemed deep enough, but as she approached she was struck by a different fear –

What about snakes? Or Creepy Crawlies?

She could hear crunching and snapping behind her now, whatever it was was still moving even though she had stopped. She chose the snakes and Creepy Crawlies. Legs first, then a slow and careful folding, like she did when she used to play hide and seek in England. She leaned back into the darkness and waited.

It was a dog.

It came out from the trees with its nose to the ground, following her scent. It stopped where she had stopped, sniffed the air, then went straight to Yinka's tree.

From inside her hiding-place, she could see its black snout flaring. Its hair was short and thick and reddish-brown. It lowered its head.

"Come out," it barked.

"No!" Yinka shouted.

"Come out," it barked again, and sat down facing the tree.

"No!"

"Very well," it said, "I can wait." And it lay down, resting its long face between its paws.

Yinka's heart raced, she was sure that the whole bush would be able to hear it. The dog seemed to stare straight at her despite the darkness of the hole. They remained frozen like this for what seemed a very long time. Then, just like that, it fell asleep. Yinka didn't dare to move or even blink, until eventually her own stinging eyes gave in and closed themselves.

She was back at home, lying down in the yard. The Woodcutter Prince kissed her and she sat up and began thinking about what she would play next. She noticed Kehinde coming through the gate from the road and she waved at him and he waved back. He sauntered over, digging his hands into his pockets, and gave her a fistful of change.

"Thank you," she said, rubbing the coins with her fingers.

He sat down next to her on the dirt. His trousers rose up and exposed the dry, cracked skin on his legs. Yinka grinned.

"You think I'm funny, eh?" he said.

"Grown-ups don't sit like that."

"Really? What do you think people sat on before there were chairs? Their heads?"

Yinka laughed.

"You're very pretty," he said, stroking her back, "much prettier than even your mother."

I am pretty? It had never occurred to her that she might be pretty. Mummy was pretty: she had long yellow hair that was straight and fine which she'd twist up into a fanned bun or allow to fall like curtains around her face and down her back, and light blue eyes like no one else's here. When they went to the market children would rush up to her and try to touch her hair or stroke her skin. Her mother would walk quickly, snapping at her father to Get A Move On. Yinka wanted her mother's eyes so much that once she dreamed that she'd stolen them and left her own brown eyes on the bedside table next to the packet of Benson and Hedges.

Now *she* was pretty, even prettier than her mother. Kehinde rubbed her thigh with the back of his hand and goose bumps appeared on her flesh. When he had gone she said it quietly to herself:

"I am pretty."

She played with the sentence, repeating it, letting the word roll out from her tongue onto her lips.

"Pretty."

"Who are you talking to?"

Yinka looked up and saw Yusuf standing above her, smiling.

"I thought you'd need these. You know your father doesn't like you walking around like a little bush girl."

He dropped a pair of flip-flops and she put them on.

"Who were you talking to?"

"No one," she said.

"Really?"

"Do you think I'm pretty?"

"Pretty, what is this pretty?" he said, laughing.

Yinka shrugged and pushed herself up, brushing the dust from her clothes. She looked up.

"The pawpaw on the lowest branch is ripe. Can you teach me how to climb and get it?"

"Yes, okay," Yusuf said, grinning down at her as she stood in the shade of the huge tree.

Yinka chuckled as he scaled up and then scuttled down the tree with ease. Still grinning, he put his hands on his hips and said,

"Looks easy, yes?"

He laughed when she nodded, and laughed even harder when she tried to climb the ridged trunk and immediately fell, bottom first, onto the clumps of prickly grass on the ground. Yinka pulled the prickles out of her dress and pursed her lips.

"That's not funny, Yusuf," she said.

"Oh, no!" he said. "I'm not laughing at you. Look, it was that bird over there, it flew down and tickled me. That's what made me laugh."

"Honest?"

He put his little finger in his mouth and flicked the inside of his cheek, making a hollow popping sound. Satisfied that this was plenty proof of his honesty, she set off again, managing to get some way this time before falling gracelessly down once more. Yusuf tried to help her up, but she pushed him away and went back to the tree. Flicking her flip-flops back off, she wrapped herself around the trunk and scaled, frog-like, all the way up, and grabbed for the pawpaw with one hand. She could see right into her house from where she was. Stretching her neck to see further in she noticed her father striding purposefully towards the door. As she struggled to get down before he got outside, the pawpaw dropped to the ground and exploded. She stopped for a moment and looked sadly down at it.

"Get down, come on. Don't worry, I will catch you," Yusuf shouted up to her.

She scurried the rest of the way down and Yusuf caught her at the bottom. They both looked up to see her father staring down from the balcony.

"Up here, now."

She tried to hold Yusuf's hand as they went inside but he gently patted it away.

"It's okay," his hand said to hers.

Her father turned to Yusuf and clipped him around his head.

"Boy, Big for Nothing, have you no common sense at all?"

"Master, sorry," said Yusuf.

"Sorry is not good enough. Get out of my sight, before I

make you sorrier than you've ever been in your life."

Yusuf slunk away.

Yinka's ear burned as her father pinched it and dragged her to her bedroom. Then he took off one of his sandals and slapped her on the thigh with it. She put out her hand to stop him.

"You want to Make Matters Worse?" he asked.

"No, Daddy." She squeezed her eyes shut as he hit her again.

"I'm sorry, Daddy!" Yinka cried out at the third and final slap. It hurt much more than the first two.

"You'll think twice before you climb that tree again," he said.

When he left, she sat and examined the welt on her thigh. If she looked closely she could see the shape of the sole of his shoe on her skin.

Spots of blood were drying on the inside of her leg where she had grazed herself falling and she turned her attention from the welt and began picking at one with her fingernail and rubbing the blood between her fingertips. After a while she remembered that she had left her flip-flops on the grass, so she went out to get them.

The pawpaw was still there on the ground. Flies were already swarming around it and an army of little black ants were marching in for a feast. She poked a finger into the unbroken side of the flesh and licked it, then got up and patted the trunk of the tree and smiled. Then she went upstairs to get ready, because that was the day they were going to see Mama at the hospital.

Yusuf drove them to the hospital. Yinka sat in the front and her father stretched out at the back.

Her father told Yusuf to wait by the car, and they walked through the carpark to the hospital's doors. Yinka had to skip to keep up with him. He took her hand as he led her through an emergency room filled with people: men and women, sitting on the chairs, sitting on the floor; babies bawling, children whining. Flies and mosquitoes buzzed all around, and she paused and flapped at the air to stop them from landing on her.

"Come on," her father said.

They took the stairs and went all the way up to the top floor. When they got to Mama's room they were told that she had been moved and they had to go back to another ward.

Mama Wole was sitting up and chatting to Aunty Modupe when they finally found her. She raised her arms and smiled when she saw them.

"Yinka, Yinka. Come and let Mama get a good look at you."

"What's this?" Yinka asked.

"Mama is poorly, so they are giving her special medicine to help her feel better," Aunty Modupe answered.

"Mama," Yinka's father said, cupping his mother's face in his hands and kissing her on the cheek, "you look much better today, yes." He sat on the chair next to the bed.

"Where is Papa?" Yinka asked.

"Ayo has taken him back home, they are picking up some okara and moin-moin for Mama," Aunty Modupe said.

"Will we see Uncle Ayo, does that mean Ade will come too?"

"Eh, and I told him not to bother because I cannot eat anything because I have this operation!" said Mama.

"Is Ade coming?"

Aunty Modupe said, "No Yinka, Ade is at home."

"Besides, we're not staying too long," her father said.

Aunty Modupe said, "Yinka, put them down." She

looked at her watch. "They'll be on their way back by now."

Yinka put the gloves she'd found back and climbed onto the bed.

"Get down! This isn't a playground," her father said. Yinka leaned against the foot of the bed, feeling the cool steel rail on her chin. When she thought no one was looking, she poked out her tongue and licked it.

"Yinka!" he shouted again.

"Leave her Thomas, leave her, she's just a child," Mama said.

Her aunt rolled her eyes. Yinka's mother said Modupe's eyes would disappear round the back of her head one day. Mama spoke to her in Yoruba but Aunty Modupe responded loudly in English.

"It's not a man's job to be taking care of his child all the time while his wife is gallivanting in England."

Mama tried to sit up. Her voice was low despite her obvious efforts to raise it. Yinka couldn't understand what she had said, but Aunty Modupe crossed her arms and loudly sucked her teeth. Yinka's mother said she was going to lose her teeth as well.

"Mama, keep your energies for getting well," her father said softly, giving Aunty Modupe one of his Looks.

Mama sank back into her pillow and turned to Yinka, who had begun to idly re-plait the end of one of her braids.

"You must keep up with your Yoruba and be good for your daddy. Mama will be keeping an eye on you."

Yinka stopped plaiting and stroked the black and white strands of her grandmother's thinning hair.

"Come on, Yinka," her father said, "Mama's getting tired, she needs her rest."

"Did you speak to Jennifer today?" Mama Wole said.

"Yes, I did. She's very worried about you and she sends

her love and says that you'd better be well by next week because you still haven't taught her how to make jollof rice yet." He laughed. "You know Jennifer."

"Daddy," Yinka asked, "how come you don't just take Mama to the Bush Doctor to get better? Aunty says he is wise and can heal the sick."

"Eh, this is what I have to contend with?" he said, giving Aunty Modupe another one of his Looks.

Mama looked kindly at Yinka.

"Our doctors can't help me. I have a modern disease, which means that only the doctors at this hospital can help me now. Thomas, get me some Lucozade from the ice box, I think I will try a few sips now."

On the way to the car, Modupe spoke quietly to her father.

"Thomas, this operation, I am worried…"

He put his arm around his sister and rubbed her shoulder.

"Nothing to worry about, this is a routine procedure, it's very common."

They waved goodbye and went to opposite sides of the carpark. Yusuf opened the doors as they approached and Yinka jumped into the front seat.

"Seat belt," her father said, and then was quiet.

Maryam had food ready for them when they got home. After they had eaten, her father said, "I'm going back to see Mama, it might take a while as I want to speak to her doctor. Go to bed nicely for Maryam. I will see you in the morning."

Yusuf got up to go with him, but he said, "I'll drive myself."

"Yes, sir," Yusuf said.

"Maryam will put you to bed at seven-thirty. No Nonsense." He wagged his finger at her.

"Yes, I mean no, Daddy," she said.

Yinka dreamt of Mama that night.

She was barefoot and the night air was cool and damp and she walked into the bush down a dusty track that was lit by the light of the moon. She came to an old hut with a broken door and she went inside. There were strange smells burnt deep into the mud walls and she got closer and sniffed and then pressed her mouth against the dry dusty wall and licked it.

"They don't feed you at home, eh?"

Yinka looked around and saw an old man carrying a walking stick. The stick was orange-brown like the trees in the bush and it was twisted and gnarled. He walked past her and sat down.

Then, behind him, Mama walked in!

Yinka jumped up to go to her, but Mama waved a hand and suddenly she couldn't move, even though her body ached to hug her Mama.

"I've come to tell you that you should not be here," she said.

"Mama! Mama, when are you coming home?"

Mama didn't look sick anymore, but her forehead was creased; she was angry. She stepped forward and the room changed around her. Weeds sprang from the walls and the light faded.

"I don't know how you are walking amongst us, but you do not belong here," Mama said.

"I like it," Yinka said, arms folded across her chest.

"You must not come here again," Mama said.

The old man with the walking stick returned and said, "Come, she is no longer your business."

Mama turned and followed the man out of the hut. She didn't look back.

Yinka looked around and the room changed again: all that was dry now became wet. The walls gave way and softened like a biscuit dipped in tea, and it became even darker. Soon she was ankle-deep in thick mud. She desperately needed the toilet.

Suddenly she was awake. Her hands were wet and shrivelled up like the skin on the face of the old man. Her nightie was damp and clung to her skin. She jumped out of bed and tried to strip the sheets off the mattress and Yusuf appeared.

"Quickly," he said, "go into the bathroom change your clothes and I'll turn the mattress over."

Daddy came in as she was getting dressed, but he didn't look at the bed or at her. He just said;

"Your Mama has gone to Heaven."

Yinka opened her eyes. Her back was aching where it had been pressed into the hard wood, her legs and arms felt cramped, but she dared not move a muscle.

The dog was still there, napping in the sun.

10

Jennifer had already swept the balcony, the front room and the kitchen, and was been thinking about doing the bedrooms as well. Instead, she now found herself standing and staring at the pile of clothes that lay on Yinka's bedroom floor. Picking them up and putting them away briefly crossed her mind, but instead she just slumped on the edge of the bed.

When Papa Wole came in to find her, she did not get up as she usually would have, nor did he wait for her to. He strode straight over and held her in a warm, Old Spice and coconut-scented embrace.

He took her back to the front room. Thomas and Modupe were there already, and the three of them began talking quickly to each other in Yoruba. She gazed out of the window, wondering why she had been brought to join them when they knew her Yoruba was not good enough to keep up. She was awoken by Modupe's sudden switch to English.

"Thomas, come help me unload the car."

She stepped out onto the balcony and watched as Thomas appeared by the car. Its boot was already open and being emptied of crates and boxes, but he went instead for the side door, pulling out two holdalls from the backseat.

"Ah. Money."

Jennifer began to sob. Her father-in-law appeared beside her.

"We will need more police, and these people won't do anything for nothing."

"Even if it's to look for a ten-year-old girl," Jennifer mumbled.

"Come and sit down," he said.

Only three days before, she had stepped off the plane and been swallowed back up into the Nigerian heat. She remembered swatting at the flies with her passport and the feeling the humid air filling her lungs. She had walked down the steps slowly, each step a punishment for her boasting to her family in England, "In Lagos, it never rains. Every day, we wake up to blue skies and sunshine."

Even so, she had felt glad to be back home.

She passed a soldier. At the smell of his cigarette she slid her hand into her bag without thinking. The soldier flicked his lighter in front of her, flashing a grin full of white teeth. Smiling back, she said:

"Se o ri nkan mi wo?"

He was taken aback. His smile wilted away, and he nodded his head in respect.

Inside the airport there was no respite from the heat. The power had failed and the fans had slowed almost to a stop. Watching them only made her feel hotter, it was almost as though their turning increased the temperature. She looked around for Thomas or Yusuf as she moved through clusters of people laden with luggage and livestock. The soldiers were all awake and on guard and their stern eyes flickered through the crowds.

She looked around at the few other expatriate travellers. Some clutched at hand luggage and passports with white knuckles, others patted daintily at their faces with pristine handkerchiefs in a vain attempt to mop up the streams of sweat. Instead of joining the orderly queue these, her own people, had formed, she weaved gracefully through the agbadas and Chanel suits and ducked past leather handbags and cages of flapping poultry, finally pushing in towards the front of the 'British Passports' queue. This small victory lessened her impatience a little. Pleased with herself, she lit another cigarette and waited.

Having passed through customs, she looked again for Thomas at the entrance, but he wasn't there. There was an argument going on outside between a taxi driver and a woman carrying a baby, and everyone was getting involved. She couldn't understand what they were saying – the language sounded like Ibo – and she decided to stay inside to wait. There was nowhere to sit, so she perched on her case and lit yet another cigarette. The electricity had come back on and the fans slowly groaned to life. This prompted a loud cheer from everyone except Jennifer, who sat alone, blowing puffs of smoke and watching the white-grey clouds linger in the air, away from the doors so as not to attract attention from the taxi drivers, hawkers and tour guides.

"Sorry, my dear. How long have you been waiting?"

Thomas cupped her face in his hands and planted a kiss on her lips.

"Bloody ages. Traffic?"

"Bumper to bumper all the way."

"Where's Yinka?"

"At home with Modupe."

"Is she OK?"

"The last three days have been hell. She hasn't eaten."

"Yinka?"

"No, Modupe. Yinka's fine, Jennifer. You know children,

they're very resilient. I've explained that Mama has gone to heaven and—"

"I should never have gone away without her."

She lit another cigarette and marched outside, ignoring the drivers who tried to intercept her, and Thomas had trailed behind with her luggage.

Jennifer blinked. What she would give to wind time back to three days ago? She stared over the edge of the balcony at Mr Segun's son, who was carrying two dining chairs through the front gate. He nodded at her and she suddenly she felt vulnerable, as though she was being watched from every direction. She sat down with her back against the mosquito screen and began to cry again.

" Where is she? Where? Why have they taken her and what are they doing to my baby?"

Her sobs drowned the remainder of her words, but the questions still hung in the air, thicker and more urgent than the promise of rain.

11

Maryam was still watching for Kehinde when she saw the two newest police cars stop outside the compound. The neighbourhood children rushed to surround them, even some adults came and stared. She did not want to see Kehinde, but his absence was making her nervous. Unable to remain still and uninterested in the spectacle, she picked up the broom and began sweeping the floor, brushing in every crevice of the room and driving the piles of dirt and dead insects to the door and out of the house. She paused often to look through the window to check again for Kehinde. She also looked occasionally towards the door, hoping to see Yusuf and hear news of Yinka. Silly child.

After a little while, she heard the squeak of the compound's front gates and looked up. It was Mr Wole. He was not dressed in his usual smart weekday attire, today he wore a green tie-dye top and casual trousers. Not wanting to speak to him, she retreated deeper into the house and sat down at the table. She turned her chair towards the window and slowly sipped her long-cold coffee.

She was still sitting there when she heard the heavy steel-capped boots of the two policemen striding up the gravel path, then a fist pounding on the screen door.

"Yes sir?" she asked through the mesh door.

"We want to ask you some questions about the missing girl, Yinka Wole."

Without replying, she unhooked the latch and stepped out into the light, closing the door behind her.

"When did you last see the girl?"

"Last night, I cook for the family."

Maryam didn't look up, and began picking at a thread on the pocket of her dress. The shorter of the two policemen said, "Did you speak to her?"

She carried on looking down, unravelling the seam and winding the thread around her fingers.

"Answer me, woman. The father tells us that you are her friend."

"No. I'm not her friend. I cook for the family, she's their child. She sometimes follows me around."

The pocket had come loose now, a perfect square of cotton in her hand. She could think of nothing else to say. She didn't know where Yinka was. She stared at the photograph of Yinka that the taller man held and her abdomen hardened; she felt a twisting inside, like a snake uncurling in the pit of her stomach.

They pushed past, leaving Maryam outside. She picked up the broom and began to sweep the front porch, determined to keep herself busy. They came back out seconds later, nodded at her, and left. She wiped the sweat from her brow, relieved they had gone before Kehinde had returned. She carried on sweeping the spotless concrete steps, torso curved around the broom's long wooden handle. Her body filled with tears, but she could not allow them to fall. Then she uncurled herself from the broom and stepped into a memory.

She had been walking back from the market and a man that her family had known for years had seen her and given her a lift home.

"Was that Edgar?" Kehinde asked.

"Yes, Uncle, he gave me a lift from the market," Maryam said, holding up the bags in her hands.

He slapped her and she dropped the bags. He slapped her again and again until she was on the ground. Then he began to unbuckle his belt. Tears spilt down Maryam's cheeks.

"You can cry blood. Get in position."

She pulled herself up, body shaking. Kehinde stood by the dining table and was fiddling with his belt buckle.

"What you thinking, eh?" He flicked the belt's tip with his thumbnail.

"Nothing," she said, keeping her head down, uncertain of what she had done wrong this time.

"You talking all buddy, buddy with the police?"

He struck her arm with the metal buckle. Maryam looked up. Thinking this was all a mistake, she smiled carefully and said,

"Uncle, that was Edgar."

Kehinde's belt stung as it hit the side of her neck and she fell against the back of the chair. He snapped the leather so that it cracked like a beef bone being separated from its joint.

"That pig! And you taking rides from the very pigs who killed your parents eh?"

Maryam took a deep breath and said, "But Uncle—"

"But Uncle," Kehinde mimicked. "You forget the people who killed your parents eh?"

"No, No!" Maryam cried.

"Pull it up, pull it up," he said.

Maryam lifted up her dress and pulled down her underpants. Turning away from him she bent over and gripped the back of the chair, slipping her fingers into the mould of her own hand that already lay between the foam-covered frame and the cushion. He beat her with the belt a few more times, then she heard it thud on the floor. The slide of his trousers' zipper followed, and she leaned forward onto the tips of her toes and held her breath.

"Good, good," he said. She felt the sofa slide and spread out her toes to keep herself from falling forward.

She stepped back into today and onto the doorstep, digging her fingers into the top of her thigh until she could breathe again.

Yinka.

Where was she? Could Kehinde have stolen Yinka as well? Steal a child? How many times had she watched Kehinde from the Wole's kitchen, following Yinka around, standing over her? She'd seen him give her money and sweets, had even felt jealous as she watched them together, wishing he could be as kind to her, the way he had been before her parents died.

"God forgive me" she breathed into herself, and suddenly her hands fell and the broom dropped to the floor. She thought that she would fall too, but her body hung there.

12

Yinka groaned as she opened her eyes and tried to move. She peered out of the hole. The dog was gone. She slipped quickly out on all fours, then tried to stand up and walk, but the ground tipped and the trees whirled. When she tried to reach for something to hang on to there was nothing and she fell back to the ground.

How long had she been hiding inside the tree?

Perhaps she should stay here on the ground, she thought. Let the beetles, mosquitoes, and bull ants march over and swarm around her, eat her away. Maybe Daddy was right, maybe God was Cruel. If He wouldn't help her, she would have to ask the only other person she knew was in Heaven.

"Dear Mama, help me Mama, please."

The dog suddenly appeared again.

"Follow me," it said.

"I can't," she said.

"There's no such thing as *can't*," the dog said.

"That's what Mama says. But I really can't, my feet are sore, look."

The dog came closer and sniffed at her feet, then licked them. Its tongue was cool and soothing.

"Come on," it said, "follow me."

Yinka followed the dog through the trees.

"What's your name?" she asked after a while.

"Dog," it said, without looking back.

Yinka told Dog about the time she visited her great-grandfather's farm in Ife.

It hadn't been tended since her father was a boy, and weeds had taken over most of the land so they had had to keep to a path leading from the road to the farm house. She ran alongside the group, dashing between the adults and catching pieces of their conversations, stepping on passing bull ants or stopping and kneeling in close to watch them and trap them and crunch them more easily. Her father and uncle, with sticks in their hands to arm themselves against grass snakes, walked ahead of the rest, stamping their feet on the ground. Daddy said they were 'testing the solidity of their legacy', but Yinka hoped they were actually helping to keep the snakes away. They talked about grown-up things as they walked: building houses and planting vegetables and making homes for their children and grandchildren. When her mother arrived, she had drifted back to listen to Aunty Modupe's stories about their grandfather who had owned and tended the land and lived in the farmhouse that he had built with his own hands. She had seen the house earlier, all that remained was a frame of rotten wood and rusty nails and hinges.

The day was hot and very humid, and her mother complained that she needed a cold Drink With Ice.

"It's not like you'll actually build on that land," Mummy said. "I don't see why you have to drag me and Yinka with you?"

Daddy had said, "It took Blood, Sweat and Tears to keep that farm going and he did, right up until the day he died."

"That land would fetch enough money to buy our own

house in England," she said. Daddy got cross and said he would not Entertain The Idea and then her mother said, "Well you must be planning to live a long time after I die because you'll be living there on your own."

Yinka told Dog she was happy her father was going to live a long time. And apart from the bull ants, she liked the farm, there was plenty of space to run.

Dog had dropped back and was now padding along beside her. She scratched her head and nodded. Her hair, which had only yesterday been in neat braids from her forehead down to her neck, was now loose and all the beads had fallen out.

"Tell me what your country is like," Dog said.

Last time Yinka had been back to England, she'd had a head swarming with lice. By the time this had been discovered, however, they had already spread to all of her cousins and their friends.

Granny Stewart was disgusted.

"Them bloody nits are much worse than the ones you get over here. I'll bet our Sue will have to get some penicillin she's so sick, and her Jimmy and Stephen have got them, too."

Yinka had sat in the living room of their three-bedroom semi-detached council house trying desperately not to scratch. Her father whispered to her, "It will be on the front page of the Evening News: 'Nigerian Lice Epidemic in Tile Hill'. Next time Yinka, see if you can carry some of our mosquitoes in your hair."

When the lice were finally gone, her mother left her in the hairdressers at the mercy of two women with lots of lipstick and big hair while she went shopping.

Her mother had said, "Just a trim."

One of the women began dry-combing her hair. Her hair did not fall downwards as they expected. Instead, every curl sprang straight back when it left the comb's plastic teeth. Yinka sat patiently, a sticky nylon apron tied around her neck.

"Have you a pair of shears handy, Dor?" The other woman giggled and came over to look at Yinka.

"Poor thing," Dor said.

Yinka looked at her own image in the mirror and then tried to concentrate on the glossy magazine cut-outs taped to the wall in front of her, the slick hair styles, perfect flicks on perfect fringes falling onto perfect faces. Flicks not frizz. The woman called Dor stood and watched her as though she was an animal at the zoo.

"Look at this Dor, think I've invented a new hairstyle?"

The hairdresser had cut the hair on one side of her head into a short neat afro. On the other side she had left an unruly hedge of combed-out curls. Dor came closer and rubbed the strands of Yinka's hair between her fingers.

"Oh, it's quite soft isn't it, I've always thought their hair was wiry. You know, a bit like a Brillo Pad," she said, as Yinka watched her in the mirror.

Yinka looked back at the pouty, smiling-and-yet-not-smiling women on the walls, and then looked down at her own fingernails, bitten down to the soft flesh of her fingertips.

Their shrill voices were still sniggering behind her when an elderly woman had spoken up from under one of the hairdryers across the room.

"For Christ's sake Sandra, she's got ears you know. Look! Now you've gone and upset her."

"How were we to know? Come on pet, I was only kidding," Sandra said, and started cutting the hair on the other side of Yinka's head.

The woman said, "That's as may be, but don't forget who brought her in, she's a Stewart and they're a bit funny about this one."

Dor looked at Sandra and raised her eyebrows. "Well, I wonder why."

"Well, my John saw the state of little Billy-what's-his-face from the Tanyard Farm estate. Last week it were. The kid's only about ten now..." The woman shifted under the dryer, adjusting her rollers.

"That boy's never ten, more like fifteen."

"Well, anyway, he chased this one all the way down to the train station. He was only playing, he didn't realise she was that young, they all tend to look older than they are, don't they? Well, anyway..."

A twig crunched loud under her feet.

"I don't want to talk about that anymore," Yinka said to Dog.

"Shame, I wanted to hear about how you escaped the clutches of an evil troll," said Dog.

Yinka and her mother had walked up The Crescent to see her Aunty Janet the week before. After dinner Yinka played with her cousin Sally outside. It was cold and their jackets were zipped up as far as they would go but the icy wind had still bitten at their hands and ears.

Sally's new bike had a pink plastic basket on the front and pink and white tassels on the handlebars. Yinka begged to have a go on it.

"Only if you promise you'll be my best friend forever and

you'll go in and ask my mum if we can have another biscuit."

"Ok."

Yinka ran straight back outside and grabbed the bike from Sally. She rode around the cul-de-sac and all the way down the hill to the end where the STOP sign was.

"It's my turn now!" Sally shouted down.

"I've only just got on," she shouted back, carrying on towards the paper shop. She had planned to go back when she reached it, but when she had got there she looked behind and Sally hadn't caught up yet, so she decided to go further and turn back when she reached the train station despite the numbness in her fingers from the cold.

A boy with a short spiky head of hair started walking towards her. He was wearing faded blue jeans which stretched across his ankles and narrowed down to nothing, and Doc Marten boots with frayed laces. His face was covered in spots, and a few blond hairs were sprouting from his chin.

"Let's have that?" he said.

"No."

Yinka stopped the bike, holding it upright with the tips of her toes as she tried to turn around. He grabbed the handlebar with one hand and pushed her off with the other. Then he ripped the pink tassels off and threw them down beside her.

"Monkey girl," he said.

She stood up and kicked his leg as he tried to mount the bike.

"Fucking jungle bunny!" he screamed, reaching down and rubbing his shin. "I'm gonna fuckin' batter ya."

Yinka got up and started to run as fast as she could, hearing his breath over the churning of the bike chain behind her. She ran underneath the bridge and into the subway that led to the train station. The subway smelt of wee and bleach, and a long pool of rainwater ran all the way down its middle. She could hear the swish-swish of the water as he rode through it, whooping and screaming, the echo of his voice ringing in her ears.

She ran into the train station and up to the ticket office but it was closed, so she ran back out into the carpark. The boy chased her around it, getting closer and closer.

Then he dropped the bike and ran at her. She tried to run past him but he wouldn't let her, he kept jumping forward, goading her.

"Shouldn't you be up a tree eating a banana?" He waved his arms and jumped up and down like an ape as he circled her, getting closer and closer. She knew that soon she would have to close her eyes and either let him hit her or fight back, and she still didn't know which one it was going to be.

She took a deep breath, turned and ran as fast as she could back towards the entrance to the railway station. She looked back to check where he was and there was her uncle coming out of the subway and charging towards the tight-jeaned boy. The boy had seen her uncle and tried to run away, but he wasn't quick enough. Her uncle held him up by his jacket lapels and roared

"Can't find anyone your own size to pick on, eh?"

Then he lifted the boy up higher still so that his frayed laces dangled above the ground.

"Well, here's something for you to think about."

Yinka had watched as her uncle let go of him and dropped his head down onto the boy's face in the same movement. She had seen her Daddy do it with a football many times but never on a person. The boy fell to the floor and looked up at Yinka's uncle

"And there's more where that fuckin' came from. Go on, get lost."

The boy ran with his head down towards the subway, and her uncle walked up to her and patted her on the back.

"Alright? Not a word to your mums." He winked at Sally and Yinka. He smelt of the house they'd spent the afternoon in: roast beef and gravy and beer and cigarettes. Sally picked up her bike.

"I'm sorry," Yinka had said to Sally, out of breath.

Sally had shrugged. "S'ok. Did you see all that blood?"

"Listen." Dog stopped suddenly and sniffed the air.

At first Yinka couldn't hear anything. Then, quietly, but getting louder, came the sound of water. She looked around to try and see where it was coming from, but she couldn't work it out. Dog started moving again so she followed him. The ground began to slope downwards and the trees cleared and then she saw that the slope led to a river. When they reached the bottom, Dog said,

"Small sips, not too much at once. Use the mud to cover yourself and follow the river, but keep close to the edge. Do you understand?"

She nodded. "But where are you going?"

"I'll be back. Follow the river," he said, and ran back up to the trees and disappeared.

The river was shallow water streaming between mud banks that had lines where the water had once been higher. Yinka carefully pressed her feet into the mushy red mud, looking around. She walked to the edge of the nearest bank and scooped some water and threw it greedily into her mouth. As the water slipped down her throat she felt a sharp pain in her stomach. She retched, and the water she drank came back up. She tried again, slower this time, sipping like Dog had told her to, trying not to disturb the earth as she scooped. Then she dug up some of the mud closer to the edge and smoothed it over her hands and arms. It felt cool and soothing on her sweaty skin and dried quickly, leaving a cracked layer of red.,

Yinka didn't want to think of those days, the day her hair was a hedge and the day before when she was chased by tight-jeaned boy. She tried to remember a time when she didn't recall anything, when she didn't think about past or present; when she didn't have the sick feeling in her belly all the time, when she wasn't lost. She looked down at the riverbed. The water she had drunk was swishing about in her belly and the shadows on the ground were getting longer.

Yinka started to walk. The path was easier near the river.

"Won't be long before it's dark," Dog said, appearing next to her.

13

There could be no forgiveness from God, Maryam thought.

She had given up on waiting for Kehinde. She could not sweep the house any more without hearing her uncle's voice in her head:

"Maryam, every morning you sweep the step and every morning I wonder if there's any step left."

So, she had decided to stop. She now sat in the corner where she usually slept with her hands over her ears, but still his sneering voice spoke in her memory:

"Just put this powder in their food and they won't wake up."

She had shaken her head and winced, expecting him to slap her, but no slap had come. He simply nodded and went on:

"Bo carries a gun. Anyone who sees him will not live to tell about it, you understand. And take that filthy Hausa out to the party with you, I see the way that boy looks at you."

He had spat as he spoke of Yusuf, then slipped on a shirt without buttoning it up. Maryam had cupped the envelope in her palm and lowered her head. She was helping them stay safe, Bo was a mad man, everyone said so. Then another thought: she would be able to go to the party, with Yusuf.

When had she started to like him? For the first few

months that Yusuf worked for the Woles, Maryam avoided him. She was naturally suspicious of him, he was a Hausa and from the North. Kehinde had said:

"Those people, they are filthy, Godforsaken people, hawkers selling food only good enough for dogs, bush-men and heathens."

She had barely spoken to Yusuf, and would not allow him to eat in the kitchen with her. His dinners were made from the scrapings off the family's plates, and always served in the same dented tin bowl. She would drop it in front on him without speaking. She hadn't intended for him to eat outside, but hadn't stopped him from doing so, and so for the first month he ate his meals cross-legged on the ground in the yard.

One day Mrs Wole came through the kitchen on her way out to watch the rain.

"In England," she said, 'it rains a lot, but not like this. A bank of umbrellas couldn't hold off this rain."

Maryam had imagined delicate English raindrops falling like mist onto black umbrellas.

Mrs Wole said, "If I close my eyes, the rain hitting the ground sounds like flames crackling in an open fire. Funny that," as she walked down the stairs.

Moments later she had stormed angrily back.

"Why is Yusuf is eating under the house?"

Maryam shrugged.

"From now on he eats in the kitchen with you,"

"Yes Missis."

"And Maryam, serve Yusuf from the pots. I really don't know what you were thinking."

When had he stopped being just another Hausa to her? When did it stop irritating her when she caught him praying at the side of the compound? She knew the answer. It had been on the one day he hadn't been there and she realised she missed him.

Yusuf's gentleness and patience with the little girl mystified her, he never seemed to be frustrated by her constant questions. Yinka was such a strange-looking child too, neither black nor white. Maryam said one evening while they were eating dinner,

"You are too patient with that girl."

"Oh, she is just a child," Yusuf said.

Maryam lowered her voice. "She is very odd. She talks to herself, she has no respect for her elders, and do you see how she fights with her cousin Ade?"

Yusuf finished the mouthful of food he was chewing, then said, "You know, this moin-moin is the best I have ever eaten."

"This is the only one that you've ever eaten," she replied.

"True, but it is the best food that has ever passed my lips," he said, with one of his grins.

"Ah, don't let your mother hear you speak that!"

They both laughed. Yusuf had put his hand over Maryam's and spoken quietly in Hausa, but Maryam had shaken her head.

"I don't understand your language, what does that mean?"

"Yinka is…friendless," he had said.

But Maryam still did not care for Yinka, and last night she had done as she was told and ground the drugs into the soup and waited in the kitchen for the drugs to work and for the family to go to sleep. Mr Wole had come into the kitchen for another helping and said,

"Maryam, Maryam. Your meal was delicious, so delightful indeed. A feast of great magnitude and magnificence to behold!"

Mrs Wole had come in behind him.

"Tom, what's come over you? If I didn't know any better, I'd think you'd been drinking. I think you'd had better get to bed."

Then she had shouted back into the living room,

"You too, Yinka."

"But Mum," Yinka answered back.

"No arguing, it's been a long couple of days and I think we all could do with a good night's sleep," she said.

Yinka had groaned as she slowly made her way out of the living room, to the sound of Mr Wole's unusual serenade:

"O sleep, O gentle sleep. Nature's soft nurse, how have I frightened thee, that thou no more wilt weigh my eyelids down and steep my senses in forgetfulness?"

"I don't think you'll be having any trouble sleeping tonight, love."

Mrs Wole had gently pushed him towards the door. She turned to Maryam and said, "It's been really tough on him, you know, with Mama and everything."

Maryam had nodded. "Yes Missis."

"The beef soup was a little salty tonight, I'm ever so thirsty. Be a love and pour us another one."

She had dropped her tumbler on the counter and its thick glass bottom had vibrated like a spun coin for a second before coming to a stop. She tucked a long blond strand of hair behind her ear and yawned.

"Yes, Missis," Maryam had said.

Maryam paced the kitchen, taking her time washing the saucepans and scrubbing the stains off the work surface.

Jennifer had called out to her;

"Maryam, go home. I'll finish up. You've done enough today."

"Nearly finished, Missis," Maryam had said.

She made the drink much stronger than usual and was relieved when Mrs Wole had finally started to fall asleep in her chair. She eventually pushed herself out of her seat and stumbled to the bedroom, not noticing Maryam still standing in the kitchen.

Maryam had gone into the living room and looked around. She had examined the copper coffee table in the centre of the room, admiring the detail of the beautiful map of the world etched into its copper top, the copper top that was cleaned and polished by Yusuf, day in, day out. She traced the outline of Nigeria with her finger and then looked for Great Britain, where Mrs Wole was from. Maryam could not understand why they would choose to live in Nigeria. Her teacher at school had told them:

"You must study in England, because, you know, all the roads are paved with gold."

Maryam had straightened up. She listened quietly for any sound coming from the bedrooms, and, satisfied that the three Woles were asleep, she had left, shaking her head and thinking, "They deserved to be robbed. All these things they have, television, stereo, radio, money for nothing. All their money and book-smarts, and yet they are still so stupid." She had closed the door quietly behind her.

This morning Maryam had been certain that the mischievous girl was hiding somewhere in the compound, but now she wasn't so sure. She felt agitated, so she stood up and decided to do some washing.

She went into Kehinde's room to collect his dirty clothes. The smell of his after-shave was even more overpowering there, and the stench of beer and stale body odour hung with it in the air. The smells pervaded the room, they clung to the blankets and the thin mattress in the corner underneath the window, the same mattress her parents used to sleep on. She opened the window to let in some air and began picking up his clothes from the floor and bundling them up under her arm.

She stopped and looked around. Almost every trace of her parents was gone. All except for the old mattress and the trunk that Kehinde now used to stack bottles of fake or black-market aftershave on. She removed them carefully and opened up the trunk and the smell of mothballs wafted into the room, mingling with the other smells. She was familiar with the carefully folded agbadas that greeted her first, they had belonged to her father. Kehinde had worn one of them, a white one, at her parents' funeral. That was almost five years ago. Her parents had been buried in the village near Ife where they had grown up. Maryam had expected to go to live with her mother's sister who worked at the University after that, but Kehinde had insisted she return to Lagos with him. Maryam had heard him arguing with them:

"Kehinde, what will you do with a child of her age? She's nearly 12. She needs a woman, a family to look after her."

Kehinde had been adamant.

"My brother would want me to see that she is well looked after. He has left her enough money to graduate high school. This is my responsibility."

Maryam had watched and listened unnoticed from the next room. Kehinde had towered over them, tall, strong so much like her father.

"You, you, who can barely manage to feed yourselves on your teacher's wage."

He had laughed then, accusing them of wanting to get steal her education funds for themselves. When Kehinde walked off her aunty had cried. Maryam had stayed long enough to hear her say quietly,

"God help that child."

She pressed the thick, woven cotton against her cheek and rubbed the silk cuff between her fingers. The scent of her father had been long lost to the mothballs, but she could remember him wearing them and that was enough. Buried beneath the clothes there lay a cardboard shoe-box filled with old school composition books. She remembered her mother helping her to cover them with brown paper many years ago.

When they had first arrived back in Lagos, Kehinde had told Maryam that her aunt and uncle were trying to steal her parents' money. He kept saying,

"Your parents would have been rich if not for that scrounging family of hers. Money for this, money for that. It's a wonder your parents had enough to feed themselves."

When she begged Kehinde to let her go to the mailbox with him, he told her,

"Don't expect anything from that good for nothing aunt of yours. Don't expect her to write. There will be no letters now that they can't beg money off you."

She shut the trunk and returned to the pile of Kehinde's washing, sorting through his sweaty-collared shirts, and picking through the trouser pockets. When she'd sorted through almost all of it something out-of-place caught her eye: there, at the bottom of the pile, was a small white vest.

14

The river bank had begun to slope downwards. Yinka's legs ached and the heat of the sun bore down on her head. She found a little shade and sat down to rest. She examined her grubby legs and arms and pressed tentatively down on the gash on her thigh. She'd never imagined that she could so desperately want a bath; she wouldn't even mind Aunty Modupe scrubbing her clean, like she had a few days before.

"Hands up for Jesus," she had said.

Yinka had sleepily raised her arms and Aunty Modupe gently pulled her nightie over her head. She had squealed as she was helped into the cold, empty bath tub, then again when she dipped her hand into the bucket of steaming water Modupe had brought and placed beside her.

"Aunty, it's too hot," she said, quickly withdrawing her hand.

"It needs to be hot to clean you. Do you want to go around smelly all day?"

She dunked an orange sponge into the water and rubbed it on the bar of soap until it was covered in white foam, then scrubbed Yinka awake.

After they had got her dressed, Yinka followed her aunt into the kitchen. Through the hatch into the parlour she could see her father standing with Papa. Mama was inside the coffin beside them.

Aunty Modupe had passed her a bowl full of cornflakes.

"Can I have some sugar on them please Aunty?" she asked.

Modupe dipped a teaspoon into the pot of sugar and then paused.

"Your Mummy puts sugar on your breakfast?"

Yinka shrugged. Modupe sucked her teeth and sprinkled a generous amount of sugar over the milky mush.

"Go in the dining room to have your breakfast," she said.

From the dining room she had still been able to see all the adults gathering around the coffin. Yinka heard Papa telling Mama who would be coming to her funeral, he'd spoken to her as though she was just sleeping. He said that The Prince was coming all the way from their village to Lagos to pay his respects.

He had spoken to her about the Old Days, when he was in the army, when she was pregnant with Modupe, the life they created and lived together. He gave her messages to take with her to the afterlife: so many vigils before, for his own father, his mother, his brother and then there was the funeral they could not attend, according to tradition. Two tiny boys who had not lived past the first month.

Aunty Modupe quietly handed Papa a cup of tea.

The adults stood together surrounded by silence. They seemed to carry it between them, their bodies were weighed down by it.

Then Uncle Ayo had stepped in between them, rolling his thick platinum Rolex up and down his forearm.

"We must not forget to celebrate Mama's life," he said.

Her father turned to face his brother.

"Perhaps if she had lived a longer life Ayo, but what is there to celebrate?"

"Our mother had a rich and full life. She gave her husband three children and lived to spoil her grand-children—"

"Celebrate, though?" her father interrupted. "I still can't believe it. It was meant to be a simple procedure and now she's dead. How can we celebrate?"

Ayo put his hands together.

"My brother, it was the will of God,"

He opened his hands and held his palms towards his brother. Ayo was an accountant, but sometimes he seemed more like a reverend, and Yinka had heard him say many times that he had considered the priesthood as a young man. Even from the dining room she was able to make out the dark brown lines across his palms, the finer lines that slithered down from his fingers. He often held his hands out in this way, as though the will of God somehow resided in their grooves. Her father cleared his throat like he did when he was arguing with her mother and shook his head slowly, then looked back down at Mama.

"God works in mysterious ways," Ayo had gone on.

Her father turned back to face his brother and said, "Look around you, open your eyes. Our God, this God you speak of is Cruel."

The word Cruel vibrated towards her.

"Ikeolu, England has softened your brain," Uncle Ayo said as he moved round and looked into the coffin.

Yinka watched him at him, the word 'Cruel' still ringing in her ears.

Then Aunty Modupe said, "Jennifer won't appreciate your lateness. Yusuf will drive you, he's in the car already. Come on, you know Lagos traffic."

Her father waved to Yinka as he got into the car.

"I'm going to pick up your Mummy," he'd said.

"Can I come, can I come?" she shouted, jumping up.

He shook his head, slammed the door, and rolled down the window as the car backed out of the driveway.

"He won't be long, finish your breakfast. I'll do your hair," Aunty Modupe said.

Yinka pushed the bowl of soggy cornflakes away and begun to pull apart her braids, catching the beads in her other hand. She enjoying the clicking sound the beads made as they tumbled against each other.

Aunty Modupe went to replace the incense, moving slowly, as though her legs were too heavy, and Yinka worried that maybe everyone would get sick like Mama. Could she have passed her sickness on before she died? Was Aunty Modupe sick? Might she get sick too? Aunty Modupe called her and she dropped the beads and watched them scatter, catching them just before they rolled off the table. She picked up her bowl and followed her aunt into the kitchen.

"You're not hungry today?"

Yinka shrugged.

"How come everyone's talking to Mama when she's not going to wake up anymore?"

"She can hear us Yinka. Yes, yes she can."

"Why does Uncle Ayo always call Daddy Ikeolu?"

"Because that is his name."

"But my Daddy's name is Thomas."

"Yes, Thomas is his Christian name, but his Yoruba name is Ikeolu. Now, no more questions, okay?"

Yinka followed her aunt back through the house. As they passed the room where Mama was, Aunty Modupe grabbed her hand and took her to the casket, and Uncle Ayo slipped his hands under her arms and lifted her up over it. Yinka's body tensed and she'd tried to wriggle away but he tightened his grip.

"No!" she screeched.

"What are you scared of? This is Mama, what do you have to say to her?"

She turned her head away. Papa took one of her hands. "Mama loves you very much. She will always look after you, even when she is in heaven," he said.

It was the first time she had seen Mama since that day at the hospital. The dead woman in the coffin hadn't looked like Mama. Daddy said Mama was in a peaceful sleep but she hadn't looked peaceful or asleep. Her face was covered in a dusty powder, and a pinkish blusher had been rubbed onto her cheeks. A gold crucifix hung from a fine gold chain around her neck, Christ's tiny golden feet resting in the hollow of her throat, and in her right hand was a white leather Bible.

"No." She tried to push herself free from her uncle's hands. "That's not Mama." Then she started to cry, but he still would not let her down.

"This is your Mama, the Angels will take her to heaven," he said.

The two men began speaking in Yoruba. Ayo softened his grip and put her down, ruffling her hair, then Aunty Modupe led her onto the veranda.

She had not been as vigorous as usual. Her strong hands, that usually pulled and stretched Yinka's hair so tight she thought she wouldn't ever be able to close her eyes again, were oddly slow and heavy. Yinka sat between her aunt's legs and even her thighs had not embraced her as tightly as usual. She hadn't tapped her sharply with the comb when she wiggled or moved her head. In between sniffing and blowing her nose, her aunt sang softly, "All things bright and beautiful, all creatures great and small. All things bright and wonderful, The Lord God made us all."

Finally, she said, "All finished. Good girl"

"Mummy, Mummy, Mummy!"

Yinka had seen the car approach the tall metal gates and ran through the house, trying not to look as she passed through the living room. She pushed past Papa and Uncle Ayo and launched out of the front door, jumping down the veranda steps two at a time. She wrapped her arms tightly around her mother's waist as she stepped out of the car.

"You'll break a leg flying down those stairs one of these days. Look at you! Oh, I have missed you," Mummy said, squeezing her tightly.

Her grand-parents' house had begun heaving with people as the morning rolled on, most of whom seemed to know Yinka even though she did not recognise them. She had had to crawl under the dining room table to get through the house. Her father caught her trying to steal away and play outside.

"Yinka, don't get dirty in those clothes, we'll be leaving for the church in a couple of hours."

"Yes, daddy."

Uncle Ayo's wife and their son Ade arrived, and she was good and waited for Ade to get out of the car and follow his family inside the house. It was his turn to pay his respects to Mama, which he could do without having to be carried. He made his way past the crowd of embroidered white, pulling the sleeve of her blouse as he passed. She shrugged him off and continued watching her parents: her mother's arm around her father's shoulder, her hand stroking the back of his neck.

Papa began a prayer and everyone bowed their heads. Afterwards, Papa and another older man lowered the lid of the coffin. Yinka watched her father slump forward as it went down. He rested his hands on the glossy white top and let out a high-pitched sigh. She felt a sharp pain in her throat as she watched him sobbing soundlessly and she'd turned away. Ade was staring at her.

He whispered, "Cry baby, cry baby," then ran out of the room. She went after him with clenched fists, speeding up once she was out of the adults' sight. She caught up with him and tried to hit him but missed. He laughed.

"Let's get some mangoes?" he said.

"I can't. Daddy says I mustn't get dirty." she said, looking up at a plump, green-yellow mango that had managed to evade the fruit bats.

"Ade, there's one," she said, pointing at it.

"Where?" he asked, picking up a stick.

"There, stupid. Are you blind?"

He looked up, squinted and shook his head.

"Give it to me."

She snatched the stick and begun smacking at the branch. The fruit was shaken, but held.

"I see it, get your own stick!" he said, grabbing at it.

"Get another."

"No!" He wouldn't let go.

"No!"

She held tightly on and looked him straight in the eye. Ade glared back.

"Get your own," he said, slowly.

"No!" she shouted again, twisting the stick and pulling harder and flicking the sharp end at Ade's knee. Ade let go and she fell to the ground, landing on a bed of sap-sticky leaves and worm-riddled mangoes.

Ade looked down at the faint thin line where the stick had cut him and prodded at it, making it bleed.

"Ah, look it's bleeding. I'm telling on you."

He ran off, shouting, "Uncle, Uncle Thomas, Yinka hit me!"

Yinka stood up, bunched her now-unravelled skirt against her waist and marched back to the house where her father was already waiting on the veranda. Ade stood behind him, a half-smile settling on his lips that had churned as he saw his mother approaching. Yinka waited for her father to smack her but he didn't. Instead, tears had collected at the corner of his downturned eyes.

"I'm sorry, Daddy. It was an accident."

He shook his head, but didn't look at her.

"Go and see your Mummy, she's in the guest room."

Then he sighed and walked away, and Yinka did as she was told.

"What's this stuff on the back of your skirt?" her mother asked.

"Ade pushed me," Yinka answered, hoping that her mother wouldn't also notice the dirt on her smart shoes.

"Oh, did he now? It's always someone else's fault isn't it? Oh, for God's sake, you'll have to take the skirt off so I can get this sap off."

"He did push me, honest."

"No Yinka! I saw Ade's knee. Why do you always have to fight with everybody, why? And Today of All Days." She tried to scratch away at the dirt. "This isn't coming off. Wait there. Do not move!"

Yinka sat cross-legged on the bed in her vest and pants and leant against the wall. This was the room that her family usually slept in when they stayed the night. The walls were bright yellow, and the double bed almost filled the small space. The only other things in the room were a bedside table and a slim chest of drawers, on top of which sat a glass vase, filled with plastic roses. On the wall there was a picture of Mama, looking directly into the camera lens.

"You don't have any wrinkles in this picture?" Yinka had once asked Mama.

"See, that picture was taken before I married your Papa. You see these lines? All my wisdom is in these lines," Mama had replied.

Yinka's mother returned with the white cotton wrap draped over her arm. She made to lift her but Yinka pulled away.

"I'm not a baby," she said.

"Then don't act like one," her mother had snapped, then she sighed.

"Okay, now let's put this back on. It's a bit damp but it'll dry by the time we get to the church. Now best behaviour, all right? Look at the state of your hair. Oh Yinka, what are you like? Now don't go messing about because it's a Sad Time and Daddy needs you to be good."

"Why?"

"Because his mummy has died and he is very, very sad."

"Mummy? Where has Mama gone?"

"Heaven."

"Where all the dead dogs and angels are?"

"Yes, that's right."

"Can she see what we are doing?"

"Oh yes, she can, so you'd better be on your Best Behaviour."

"Can we see her?"

"It's time to go to the church now. Daddy's waiting for us."

"Mummy?"

Her mother sighed again. "That's enough now, Daddy will be wondering where we are, come on."

Her father carried the coffin, shoulders bent forward, with the other male members of the family. The row of men hunched under the weight of it. Yinka peered into the bus that had been converted into a hearse; the middle seats had all been pulled out to make room for the coffin.

"Go on, you can go and sit with Aunty Modupe and Papa," her mother said, pointing to a small space between them.

"There's no room."

"Daddy wants you to go with them."

"There isn't any room. I want to go with you and Daddy."

Yinka's mother's hands pushed her further into the hearse and Aunty held out her hand towards her, but Yinka leaned back.

"No! I don't want to!" she shouted. Papa put a finger to his lips.

"Shush, you'll wake your Mama."

Yinka looked back and saw her father.

"Daddy!" She jumped up, squeezed past her aunt's knees and leapt from the hearse, falling onto the road. Her father quickly picked her up. She dusted herself off as he dragged her with him.

"I just wanted to go with you and—" She heard mumblings and tooth sucking around her.

"Okay," he said, "Okay."

Yinka sat in the back of the car with her parents, who sat in silence, her mother's hand resting on her father's knee. The road to the church was short, but the traffic was lined up bumper to bumper ahead of the funeral procession. They were travelling so slowly that a conveyer-belt of hawkers had overtaken them. The traffic was congested and a heavily-laden bus had bellowed thick black smoke ahead and Yinka held her breath and pinched her nose until they had passed it. The traffic finally gave way and the car meandered to avoid the potholes in the road. She pressed her head against the glass and gazed out of the window. An animal lay by the side of the road, its decaying body distorted into a grotesque pose.

When their convoy came to a stop, an ambulance appeared, knocking the mirror off the car in front as it passed. The driver jumped cursing out of his car, picked it up, and threw it onto the passenger seat. There had been another bus accident, and a traffic policeman in a starched uniform and brilliant white shirt directed the traffic to around the overturned vehicle.

Her father slapped his palm on the steering wheel so hard that Yinka jumped back in her seat.

"What's the hurry? The church is going to still be there and Mama is in no rush," her mother said. "It's morbid, all these people getting out of their cars to look."

Yinka pressed her head against the glass to see what was happening and the traffic began to move slowly forward. The bus was empty. Most of its passengers had got out and begun walking, and only a few remained. A group of women huddled together and were crying as the ambulance men picked up and carried a stretcher holding a lumpy mound covered by a blood-stained sheet. A woman was selling cold Pepsis from an icebox to the spectators and a group of men dragged out something from underneath the bus.

"Today of All Days." her mother muttered.

Yinka twisted her body round to see what was happening, "Was that a dog? Did it get run over? Is he dead? Mummy, do you think the dog is dead?"

"Yes, I think it must be. Look we're moving. Come on, face forward, we'll be there soon,"

She had many more questions and she parted her lips to let them spill out, but then she saw her mother gently stroking her father's shoulder. She slumped quietly back into the seat, thinking better of it.

They arrived an hour late to the church. The driver of the hearse struggled to find a place to park; there were cars lined up on both sides of the street. Her father went straight to join the other pallbearers.

"Look at all these people," her mother said, and started to cry.

They watched as the crowd parted to let the pallbearers into the church.

Ade sat next to his mother, a few seats away from Yinka. He tried to get her attention, but her mother had said, "Ignore him."

"Ade's not sitting properly," she whispered back.

"I don't care what Ade's doing, just sit and be quiet."

Ade was still been trying to get her attention when the adults stood, heads down and eyes closed in prayer. He stuck his tongue out at her and then faced forward again, closing his eyes. Yinka felt her mother's elbow nudge her and she looked up to see her giving her one of her Looks, which Yinka knew meant that she was not to move Or Else. Yinka put her head down and closed her eyes, and her mother patted her on the back.

The doors were open and people were standing in the doorway and along the edges of the pews. Those who couldn't fit inside stood outside to pray.

When it was time, her father stood up and walked to the front to read from his own dog-eared bible. He paused and cleared his throat when he reached the front.

"But I would not have you to be ignorant,

Brethren, concerning them, which are asleep,

That ye sorrow not, even as others, which have no hope…"

Yinka peeked up at her mother, who was dabbing her eyes with a handkerchief. She turned and looked back at

Ade, who was chewing gum, pulling it out of his mouth and wrapping it around his finger and putting it back in.

"Wherefore comfort one another with these words."

Her father closed his bible and stepped down, and calls of 'amen' rippling through the church.

"Let us pray," the Reverend said, and the congregation stood and bowed their heads.

Yinka was desperate to get out of the stuffy church that day, but now, surrounded by trees and bushes and insects, she wanted more than anything to be back in it, with its old woody smell and the hard, narrow seats and with Mummy and Daddy. She could feel it slipping away.

Just a few more minutes she thought.

Let me go back for just a little bit longer.

But the church and all those in it were gone.

"And Mama's not coming back, ever," she said.

Dog nodded his head.

Yinka followed the river as the sun slid down the sky.

15

Maryam folded, unfolded and re-folded the vest, as if doing this might make it vanish, or change it somehow. She wished that she would disappear. She put it down and went outside.

Even in the sticky midday air she felt better, cleaner than she had in there, surrounded by him. She looked around the compound; most of the groups that had gathered earlier had now left to search for Yinka.

Yinka.

Waves of nausea crested in her throat and she held her breath to keep them down.

Yusuf pulled into the compound. She called out and ran to the car to meet him.

"Have you found her?" she said, out of breath.

"No."

"No?" Maryam held the vest tightly in her fist. "No," she said again, and the waves returned, drowning her. She reached out to Yusuf, as if he could save her.

"Maryam, what? We'll find her, I'm sure of it," Yusuf said.

Maryam continued to moan.

"Maryam?"

"Kehinde, it was Kehinde. He robbed the house. He took her. It's him."

"What are you talking about?"

"Yinka, she's been in the house, my house, this was in his room, it's hers. It was him and Bo, they're thieves, bad thieves. He made me put drugs in their food, I had to take you out…God forgive me, oh please. Yusuf, please forgive me."

She dropped to her knees and looked up at him, and he let go of her hand.

"What are you talking about? Maryam, where's Yinka? Where is she?" he said.

"I don't know, as God is my Witness, I don't know."

"You drugged them? Who? Maryam, what are you saying to me?" He raised his voice. "Where is Yinka?" He dragged her to her feet. "Where is Yinka?"

Maryam heard the door open and saw Mr and Mrs Wole coming down the steps with the rest of the family behind. The same policemen who had searched her house were with them.

Yusuf let her go and turned to the Woles. "She says that Kehinde robbed the house. She says that Kehinde took Yinka."

He snatched the vest from Maryam and passed it to Jennifer.

Maryam tried to stand, but a strong hand suddenly gripped the back of her neck and held her down. Mrs Wole stepped in front of her.

"Where's Yinka?"

"I don't know!" Maryam cried.

"Where is she?" Mrs Wole slapped Maryam across the face. "I saw you this morning. You said you hadn't seen her."

"Missis, I tell you, I didn't know, I didn't know until I found it."

"I sent Yinka to see you yesterday morning…"

"I was at the market. I didn't see her, I found this," Maryam said. "You don't know what he's like."

Mrs Wole screamed at her, "What are you talking about?"

Maryam covered her face with her hands. "No," she said, "no, I can't help you."

One of the policemen pulled her up to her feet by the hair and the other slapped her with the back of his hand. She felt a kick from behind, followed by a punch.

"Is it money, is it money you want—" she heard Mr Wole shout. Then Mrs Wole's voice, sounding far away, the echo of a scream.

"Where is she?"

Maryam tried to curl up in a ball but it was useless. She stopped trying to cover her stomach and face, this was what she deserved. Then, suddenly, it stopped.

"Enough!" Mr Wole shouted at the policeman who was still shaking her. He turned.

"Yusuf, take her upstairs."

Inside, Yusuf said sadly, "And so, last night…"

"I had no choice, Yusuf. He said that if you were there, he would kill you. I didn't know about Yinka." She began to cry. "Yusuf, please."

Mr and Mrs Wole came into the room.

"I know you are scared, but please, this is my baby, tell me where she is." Mrs Wole sounded calmer now, kind.

"I don't know," Maryam said. "I haven't see her."

There was a long silence. Finally, Maryam said, "My uncle, he is not a good man. When my parents died, he came to live here with me, to take care of me. He wouldn't let me live in Ife with my mother's family." She searched for the words to express what she needed to say, but her English failed her and she began to speak in Yoruba.

Modupe translated as she spoke.

"Her uncle is a drinker. He gets drunk almost every night. When he comes back after hanging out with his area boys he beats her. For no reason. Since she was eleven. He has spent the money that was left to her by her parents to finish school, and she was expelled when he refused to pay her fees. When he's drunk, and sometimes when he is not he makes her do things." Their voices overlapped, fading in and out of one another. Maryam's voice quiet and flat as she mumbled to the ground, Modupe, deeper and only a little louder, stumbling as she grasped for the right words in English.

"He has made her do these things since she was a child. Things that a man and wife do together..."

Modupe stopped translating and began to cry but Maryam went on, her words bursting wet out of her mouth, until finally she exhaled and looking up she whispered to Yusuf in English,

"I'm sorry."

16

It was five o'clock when the two policemen returned to the house. While they spoke to the couple they watched the red-eyed Maryam, who sat in the corner, staring at the ground. They spoke so quietly that even Yusuf, who stood nearby, could barely make out their words.

"The girl was right."

"...van was there, but this man Bo, was not."

Yusuf watched them watching Maryam with their puckered-up faces like they had raw pepper on their tongues. Mr Wole gestured to him to follow as they were led out of the house. Outside many other police had gathered, and, as the threat of dusk hung in the air, the neighbours who had been out searching had begun drifting back to the compound.

Mrs Wole was saying:

"I don't believe this. I don't bloody care about what's in the van. I want my daughter. Why aren't you looking for Yinka?"

The senior officer, smart jacket off and shirt soaked in sweat replied. He spoke clearly, enunciating each word;

"Missis Wole. It will be dark in one hour. Tomorrow we will search for her in the bushland, just outside Ikeja." He pointed. "We have searched the whole of Ikeja with a fine-toothed comb, inside and out. We are now looking for these men, Kehinde and Bo. When we find them we will make them tell us where she is."

Jennifer was shaking her head. "You can't stop looking. It'll be dark, what if she's lying somewhere, what if—"

The policeman turned, now addressing Mr Wole.

"Mr Wole. These thieves, the likes of this man Kehinde, they do not leave witnesses. We will search the bush tomorrow, there are many times that we find bodies."

Yusuf watched Mr Wole reach for his wife's hand. She waved it away and walked off.

The policeman continued: "We will take the girl to interrogate. She may know more than she is telling."

"She knows nothing more. She will stay with us. She is going nowhere," Mr Wole said.

The senior policeman frowned. "Mister Wole…"

"Leave her," Mr Wole said firmly. "She will still be here tomorrow."

Darkness was pouring into the sky now. The red light drained into the horizon, leaving behind a blanket of black, pin-pricked with stars.

Mrs Wole sat, knees vibrating, picking and gnawing at the skin of her fingers.

Mr Wole said, "I will go and search also, first thing tomorrow. That bush land is only a few miles from here."

"If only we had known earlier," Mrs Wole said, looking at Maryam. "She can't be dead, she can't be. I'd know, I'm sure I would feel it."

As night settled in, the last neighbours drifted back. Unable to rest in their own houses, they congregated in the Woles' compound, gathering in groups and sharing information. Word about Kehinde had spread, and a crowd had formed around his house too. Some were shouting for Maryam to show her face. The lights were still turned on in the house so people could see inside.

Mr Wole turned to Yusuf. "You will have to get her out of here." He pulled out money from his wallet and held it out to them.

"Sir, I can't leave you. Not at a time like this," Yusuf said, keeping his hands in his pockets.

"Kehinde is unlikely to return, and they will come and take her. I won't have the power to stop them." He looked at Maryam.

"Then let them take me," Maryam said.

Mr Wole said, "No. You have people in Ife. Yusuf, take her to the bus station."

"I can't Mr Wole, I can't go," Maryam said.

"You can and you will. Don't go back to your house. Go."

When they arrived at the bus stop, Maryam said, "You don't have to wait," as she got out of the car.

"No, Mr Wole asked me to make sure you were safely on that bus. He's given me money." He handed her the roll of naira.

"My aunt's name is Solomon, Yusuf," she told him as she took it.

She wrapped her arms around him and he could feel her heart beating beneath her soft skin. He watched her board the bus. She found a seat by the window and waved to him. He got back into the car and was just about to drive off when he saw Maryam jumping from the bus and running across the road.

"The bus may go without you," he said.

"I remembered that Bo has a place."

17

Darkness descended and it started to rain, big, fat splatters that slopped through the leaves and branches and down onto Yinka. There was no more birdsong. The storm had finally come and drowned out every other sound from the bush.

Yinka looked up and let the drops of water fill her mouth. She walked on, drinking like this and taking long breaths between each gulp, until the ground gave way and rolls of earth began sliding down the embankment. She fell and was swept down to the river with them and rolled along with the thick leafy branches. There was barely time to breathe between each surge that crushed down on her. She felt the bottom with her feet and tried desperately to stand but the river swelled ever deeper and she was sucked under by another wave, then thrust up for just long enough to take one deep breath before being submerged again. Each gasp of air she fought for became shallower than the last.

Then, a stillness. A forgotten but familiar feeling of there being no breath, just the rhythms and the echoes of a dream.

It was the day after the funeral. Her mother had been upset when her father had to go to work. She lay on the sofa, flicking through last month's 'Women's Own' magazine that she'd bought to read on the plane.

"I'm bored," Yinka said.

"You're always bored. Why don't you play outside?"

"Can I go and see Maryam, Mummy?" she said.

"That's a good idea, why don't you take this for her? Tell her she can keep it." Her mother handed her the magazine and she bounced out of the house with it.

Yinka went to the back of the compound to look for Maryam, but couldn't see her. She hopped up the three concrete steps to her door.

"Maryam! Maryam!" she shouted. She stepped into the house and the screen door slapped shut behind her. Her nose itched at the bitter smell of coffee and overripe bananas. One of the bananas in the bowl on the table had split and a sticky yellow-brown liquid oozed out onto the wood. She looked away and called out again.

"I think she's in her room."

Kehinde stepped out of the darkness. His grey shirt was open and his trousers hung belt-less around his hips. She noticed the bones of his hips sticking out, seeming to almost pierce his flesh.

"Come, come see her."

Yinka looked back at the front door.

"No, thank you," she said, and turned to leave.

"Come, we'll go and look for Maryam together," he said.

The light was dim but the brilliant-white half-moons of his fingernails seemed to be glowing. She shook her head. He stepped in front of her.

What was he saying?

She could see him speaking but couldn't get a hold of what he was saying. His voice was very gentle;

"Don't worry just follow me."

She followed him through the corridor stacked with dented, empty cardboard boxes – Milo, Kellogg's Cornflakes, Nestle.

The curtains were drawn but the scorching sun warmed the room through them. There was a bed in the corner, and its thin, faded blanket spilt onto the floor. Yinka looked around for Maryam but she wasn't there. She heard the door's bolt click behind her.

She knew it was hot but she was cold. Kehinde was standing close to her, so close she could feel his pulse against her.

What did he say? Good girl?

He knelt down and began paring away her clothes, the dress she was wearing, her vest, her pants. She gazed at the curtains, trying to make out faces in the pattern of the fabric. Kehinde's breathing was loud and deep and fast. She could feel his breath on her face, it smelt of mint and cigarettes. She could see some faces now, first one, then another.

She was moving, being moved.

What is he saying?

Her ears felt blocked like they did when she was on an aeroplane. Now he was standing in front of her and pushing something into her mouth and it made her gag. His laugh was warm and kind and he was rubbing her face with the back of his hand.

She was floating. Her body was moving again and her head flopped back and she saw the ceiling was moving back and forth, back and forth, back and forth.

It hurts. I'm going to get into so much trouble.

And then the ceiling stopped and Kehinde helped her up and took a towel and wiped her, down there, not roughly but not gently just naturally like he was wiping her face or her arm or her leg.

What is that red?

She groaned as she stood up but didn't recognise the sound as herself and so didn't register the pain. She was floating again.

And then she was dressed. Kehinde handed her a glass. She sipped the tepid water. Her lips were numb.

What is he saying?

He was smiling. Yinka smiled too, and politely put down her cup.

"I have to go now," she said, and pushed open the screen door and walked into the light. She stopped, half-blinded, and gripped the rail at the top of the stairs to steady herself as her eyes adjusted to the light, she thought she could see a figure sitting at the back of the yard under the tree.

It was Mama.

She can see everything now that she is in Heaven.

"Yinka? Yinka!"

Her mother was calling her from the house.

Yinka sat on the stool in the kitchen and stared at the soft, barely-cooled sponge, the bright pink sugary jam and thick cream bursting out of the middle, the thin dusting of icing sugar sifted over the top.

"Let's have a slice of that cake, Victoria Sponge. Mama's favourite too, remember?"

"Don't just look at it…"

Her mother pushed the plate closer then watched as Yinka took a bite into the slice of cake.

"Better than the last one?"

Yinka nodded and said, "Delicious Mummy. Best ever."

She finished it despite how much her insides hurt. Mummy said, "Shall we be naughty and have another piece?"

"No thank you."

She slipped off the stool and went to the bathroom and vomited. She took off her pants and tried to scrub the blood out.

"Yinka!"

Her mother was standing behind her, seeing the wet scrunched up pants in her hands.

"Oh, what are we going to do with you? Put that in the wash basket and we'll get another pair. You know pet, you're too old to be wetting your pants."

She waited until her mother had handed her a fresh pair of pants and she balled up the blood-stained ones and buried them in the bin.

Starlight.

Yinka had been thrust back up to the surface for a second; she took a deep breath before descending again. Her feet became tangled in something and she finally stopped. Her head and shoulders were above the water but the river was still slamming against her, trying to pull her under and tow her along with it.

That was when she saw her, standing there on the bank of the river. Hands resting on broad hips, dressed in the same blouse and wrap that she had been buried in. Dog was sitting patiently beside her.

Yinka struggled to free herself. She saw a knot of vines leaning into the water from the bank and grabbed hold of them. She pulled herself to the edge and dug her fingers into the mud and climbed, slowly, out of the surging water.

"Mama!" she shouted when she'd caught her breath.

"Stay there," Dog said. "Stay there."

Then, suddenly, she felt as though she was back in the river, but floating, not struggling anymore.

"Is this heaven?"

"No Yinka, this is not heaven."

18

"Oh, Lord Almighty, we pray that you bring Yinka back to us. We pray that you keep her in your Son's loving arms. That you are shielding her from pain and suffering. We pray that wherever she is, that she is safe with you. Oh, Jesus Christ Our Lord."

Papa rocked back and forth as he prayed. Thomas stood crying at his side.

"Amen, Amen," Modupe whispered from behind.

"Oh Lord Almighty, we pray that you are casting your light upon her, and in doing so, you let your glorious light lead her home. We pray that you also give Thomas and Jennifer the courage and strength that they need." Papa's voice filled the room. "We trust in you, to deliver retribution…"

Jennifer could just about hear the crickets over Papa and the thundering rain. She resented their prayers, they seemed a luxury to her. How easy it is to surrender a child to God, when that child is not your own. She wished that she could have sat next to Thomas and held his hand, perhaps through his touch he might have been able to pass his faith in Jesus on to her. She couldn't bring herself to try.

"Oh Lord Almighty, let us pray for the safe-keeping of Yinka, that she can be returned to us or be in peace forevermore…"

Modupe walked in to the kitchen and Jennifer gently closed the door behind her. Modupe busied herself; covering the leftover cooked food with foil and washing the dishes in the sink, while Jennifer picked up a tea-towel and began to dry them.

"Jennifer," Modupe said, "please let me do this, your place is in there."

"Don't tell me where my place is!" Jennifer snapped. Modupe almost dropped one of the plates.

"Pele, sorry."

Together they cleaned the whole kitchen, accompanied by the sounds of the prayers in the next room and the drum of the rain.

"Do you hear that?" Maryam said suddenly.

"What's going on out there?" Jennifer said.

Modupe opened the outside door and a cacophony of loud, angry shouts poured in with the rain. They stepped out on to the top step of the kitchen veranda and saw Ayo winding his way through the crowd. People were yelling and screaming and waving sticks, some even had bush knives. Ade was at the front, squashed between two women. He'd taken his shiny new shoes off and was trying to turn back but was being pushed back towards Maryam's house by the throng.

When Kehinde appeared at his door even the rain seemed to hold its breath. The policemen were the first to move.

"Raise your hands," they both said, pulling out their guns.

Kehinde was drunk. He stumbled and staggered this way and that, holding out his hands to balance himself.

"Move back," the policemen shouted at the people closer to Kehinde.

Ade had now been pushed right to the front of the crowd.

Kehinde faltered towards him and Ade threw both his shoes at him: one ricocheted and hit one of the policemen, and the other hit Kehinde's head.

"You filthy kid, you'll be sorry," Kehinde slurred, grabbing at him. He missed, and the two women nearest to him lunged forward. Ade fell to the ground and disappeared.

Jennifer watched as the women beat Kehinde and the people behind them surged in and took their sticks to him. The crowd became an animal, circling and pouncing on him from all sides, a thriving, single mass of flailing arms and legs beating downwards to the rhythm of the rain.

His pleas for mercy went unheard, drowned in the cracks the blows, the shouts and cries.

Then, suddenly, it was over. The night-time chorus of crickets and frogs was suddenly loud and ringing painfully in Jennifer's ears. The crowd had moved back to reveal Kehinde's lifeless body, limp and bloody and broken. The rain thrashed down on the corrugated roof of the now empty house before them.

Modupe was crying.

"Come on," she said, pulling Jennifer inside. Thomas and Papa came to the door and Thomas took her in his arms. Papa rushed down the stairs to help Ayo and Ade up in to the house.

Jennifer began to sob.

"What have they done? How will we find her, how will he tells us now what he's done with her?"

Ade ran into the house and embraced his mother who was standing in the doorway of the living room. She leaned down to hug him.

"I've lost my shoes, I've lost my shoes," he cried into her arms.

19

The bus was crowded and the rain battered rhythmically down on its thin metal roof.

In a few short hours Maryam would be with her aunt and uncle/family, and safe; safer than she had been in years.

She watched as the rain turned to a river at the road-side, carrying a selection of debris along with it: fragments of wooden crates and empty bottles, rubbish and food waste. Something larger caught her eye and she squinted to make it out and quickly turned away again. It was the small bloated body of a dog.

Her only luggage was a small bag containing her mother's dress and the money Mr Wole had given her, and this she held close. She looked out of the window in order to avoid making eye-contact with anyone.

Out of the corner of her eye she regarded the woman who sat next to her. She was snowed in to her seat by bags, and had a small hen in a wooden cage on her lap. Every time the bus bumped or veered, the bird would become agitated and would squawk and screech, gripping the bars with its feet desperately trying to peck its way out.

Focusing back on the window she noticed her fractured reflection: her lip protruded and was split and swollen, and the soft skin around her eyes had ballooned and turned a blue-grey colour. Beyond the shards of her reflection lay the darkness, the same, slick, tar-like darkness that she and Yusuf had walked home in only the night before. That same cloak of night under which they had kissed. She stared into that, avoiding the floating debris below and her broken image.

20

Yusuf had intended to drive straight back to Ikeja. Yusuf knew that it would be a waste of time trying to find the old shack that Maryam remembered, especially in this rain – and yet—

He stopped, locked the car and began to walk down towards the bank of the river, tripping and sliding as he went.

"Yinka!" he shouted, over and over.

He couldn't see the shack and was now almost sure that he hadn't come the right way. Maryam had assured him that this river was the same one which flowed through into Ikeja during the wet season but he was not certain that he would be able to find his way back even so.

"Yinka!"

A little further, he thought, just a few more minutes, and then he would make his way back up to the car. He wished he had worn his long trousers.

"Yinka!"

21

Yinka huddled close to Dog.

"Do you think anyone is looking for me?"

"Of course, you've got ears haven't you, listen."

"Yinka!"

She jumped up.

"Come on," she said, "That's Yusuf, I know it is."

22

Jennifer opened the screen door, stepped out onto the balcony and lit a cigarette. She watched as the body was thrown into the boot of the police-car, and her eyes followed the lights of the vehicle as it drove out of the neighbourhood. The rain had stopped, for now, and the moon was hidden behind light grey clouds. As she stubbed out her cigarette, she remembered that she still had not called since coming back. She watched another pair of lights appear in the distance but it was only when it stopped at their gate that she saw that was Yusuf. As she turned away to go back into the house she saw another, smaller figure, sitting in the passenger seat.

"Yinka, my baby!"

23

Yinka's mother gently washed her down with a soapy sponge. It felt like it was someone else's body being cleaned, someone else's blood and dirt flowing down the drain.

Her father came in when they were finished, carrying a bottle of tablets.

"What are they?" her mother said.

He took one out and handed it to her.

"Quinine. We'll get the doctor tomorrow, but we'll start her on a dose tonight."

"You think she's got malaria?"

He shrugged. "High temperature, vomiting…what else could it be?"

Yinka watched as the murky water disappeared down the drain.

"Get some juice, Tom."

"Where have you been?" Mummy whispered in her ear. Yinka's lips opened, but no sound came. "I can't believe we almost lost you, all day I kept thinking what would I do if, if…"

I could tell her now, Yinka thought, before Daddy comes back.

"I can't bear to think about what you've been through, what he did to you," she said.

Her father came in holding a glass of juice and she closed her mouth again.

"Here, take this, it'll make you feel much better," he said.

She felt the pill's bitterness burn the back of her tongue and scratch at the inside of her throat as she swallowed it. The sensations brought her back, closer to her body.

"Good girl," her mother said.

Her father was looking out of the window through the gap in the curtains. Her mother spoke again;

"What happened, Yinka? You can tell me."

There was a glistening in the corner of her father's eye, and as she watched a tear dropped down his cheek. The only other time she could remember seeing him cry was at Mama's funeral.

"She needs to rest," he said. He picked her up and carried her to her room.

They both sat at the bottom of her bed until they thought she was asleep, then tiptoed out.

She waited until she was sure they were no longer outside, then sat up.

"Dog, Dog are you there?" she whispered.

Dog hopped onto her bed and she patted him on the head.

"Tell me a story."

"There is an old woman..." Dog began.

As old as Methuselah himself.

She lives in the bushland, far, far away.

She lives in the no man's land where spirits of good and evil wage their wars amongst the trees, a place where only the animals are safe and few humans dare tread.

Not all men heed the warnings of the wise, and some will

venture where they are not welcome. The less foolhardy will equip themselves by wearing special stones and carrying herbs in bags around their necks. Many, however, are not wise, drunken fools, desperate girls and runaway boys, unbelievers or those with deaf ears. These people are seldom seen again.

Those who must to go into the bush will further arm themselves with the spirits of their ancestors, and only with such support can a traveller be guided through the dangers to the old woman's home.

For a traveller to return there must be someone waiting for them on the outside. The whole village must know and prepare and call out for them.

Sometimes, though, it will take days – and sometimes weeks or months – and the villagers will drift away, losing hope. They have things to do: children to feed, food to hunt, fruits and vegetables to gather. The closest family member will always wait the longest, but even they will eventually lose hope and stop calling their loved one's name.

If this happens the traveller can never return, no matter how many stones or herbs or ancestors they carry with them.

Why would a person take such a risk? The old woman has powers of healing, far greater than any medicine we know. And so sometimes the only option is to seek her and take offerings in return for her help.

In the old days before the pharmacies this was more often necessary. No one has been sent for some years now. It is sad because she is thorough. Only when a person is healed will she release them and let them follow their name home – if their name is still being called. If it is not she will send their body back down the river to their home.

One night, many years ago, the old woman heard a noise. At first she thought it was an animal, and she went outside to greet it. Soon she realised that it was like no bush-animal: this was a human's cry. She hunted around for its source, and there, entangled the leggy branches of an acacia bush, was a girl of about ten years old. The child was frightened and covered in dirt and bloody scratches. She listened out for the child's name and heard a faint call;

"Tobunko." once, and no more.

The old woman listened with hope for hours and days but she didn't hear the girls name again.

Strangely, though, the child did not die, but instead got stronger with time. The old woman thanked the Gods and kept the child.

Tobunko loved the old woman very much, and in return for her love the old woman gave her all her secrets and memories. She taught her how to hear the voices of the forest and how to use them to heal.

When the time came for the old woman to die, she began to shrink.

Tobunko, who was now a young woman, was very sad, but she knew the time had come and she had learnt all there was to learn. She knew what she had to do.

She clothed the shrunken old woman in the dress that she had been wearing when Tobunko arrived as a child, and laid her on the bed of woven palm leaves. As she prepared to release her, she saw that villagers were waiting. She heard her mother's voice calling out her name, just as it had all those years ago.

Tobunko released the old woman and watched as she floated downstream. She watched as the woman's shrivelled up skin became smooth and her body became soft, watched as the old woman turned into a child; the very same child that she, Tobunko, had been all those years ago. She watched as the boat drifted to the other side of the bank where the villagers waited. She smiled when she saw her mother embrace the old woman who had become the little girl.

Tobunko turned to go back to her hut and her back ached with the years. She held on to her stick and used it to steady herself as she walked, bent over and shrivelled, back through the bushland.

Acknowledgements

Paul, Olivia and Sebbie for their unwavering belief

Effie, Julian, Laurie, Siona and Sharon for reading those very early drafts with thoroughness and kindness

Nancy Peacock – mentor and friend, thank you for your wise teachings

Finally, I am immensely grateful to Natasha Robson and Robert Peett – for all their support, expertise and dedication.